# Reserved for
# Mark Anthony Crowder

BY ALISON SMITH

E. P. DUTTON    NEW YORK

*Library of Congress Cataloging in Publication Data*

Smith, Alison P., date.   Reserved for Mark Anthony Crowder.

SUMMARY: A sixth-grader who believes everyone including
his family thinks him odd, spends his summer tending the
family garden and cultivating his self-esteem.
[1. Family life—Fiction. 2. Gardening—Fiction]  I. Title.
PZ7.S6425Re  1978  [Fic]  78-6460  ISBN: 0-525-38199-6

Published in the United States by E. P. Dutton, a Division
of Sequoia-Elsevier Publishing Company, Inc., New York

Published simultaneously in Canada by Clarke,
Irwin & Company Limited, Toronto and Vancouver

Editor: Ann Durell    Designer: Jennifer Dossin
Printed in the U.S.A.   First Edition
10 9

To Dan and Jessie

# CHAPTER 1

Mrs. Prescott reached for the atlas. It was on the top shelf in the class library, as usual. Mark Anthony pulled himself down into his seat till his chin hovered two inches above his desk. He opened his math book and stared at the page, even though it was so close to the end of his nose the words were all blurred.

"Mark Anthony."

It was no use. "Yes, ma'am?"

"You're so nice and tall. Get that atlas down for me, would you?"

Mark Anthony groaned inside himself and stood up.

As he walked down the aisle, he could hear the words hissing out behind him. "Mark Anthony's so nice and tall."

He reached for the atlas and handed it to Mrs. Prescott.

"Thank you, Mark Anthony."

The echoes followed him down the aisle, soft and with a snigger of laughter in them. "Thank you, Mark Anthony. Mark Anthony's sweet."

He sat down, staring at his math book, feeling his face burning. Anger filled him and pounded in his ears. If only she wouldn't ask him to help her like that. She was a nice woman, and she meant well, but every time she called on him like that, the kids gave him the needle. Besides, he wasn't the only tall kid in the sixth grade. Lots of the girls were almost as tall as he was. But no—every time—"Mark Anthony, you're so nice and tall . . ."

It hadn't helped that he'd always gotten good grades, either. It had made it worse. So, for the last six weeks he'd been really coasting—not much homework, no more speaking up in class, and no great effort on tests. Mrs. Prescott had noticed. She'd made a couple of comments about mental laziness and glanced in his direction.

The bell rang, and he got up instantly. He could go home. He gathered up all his books and headed out the door, toward the school-bus parking area.

Earl Jones caught up with him in the corridor. Earl was short. He was lucky. And he didn't have to wear glasses—thick ones, like headlight lenses. Doubly lucky. He was Mark Anthony's best friend, his only friend, really, at school, and Mark Anthony had moved to Ridgedale a year ago.

"Let's fool around for a while before we go home. The guys are getting up a softball game."

"OK," Mark Anthony said, and felt his stomach tighten with apprehension.

"I'm going to catch for Brian's team. Come on."

Mark Anthony followed Earl as he slipped through the crowds in the corridor.

Outside, the spring sun was hot and blindingly bright, after the dim coolness of the school halls.

Mark Anthony set down his jacket and his books in a corner of the playground and followed Earl out to the softball diamond. The fellows were choosing up sides. This was the part he hated—the very worst part.

"Mark Anthony will be on our team," Earl said to Brian. "He can hold down first base."

Brian spat on the dusty ground.

"No way. We don't need another man."

"Yes, we do," Earl insisted. "Put Mark Anthony on first."

"Tommy's going to play first. At least he can see the ball coming."

"I can see," Mark Anthony said. "Nothing's going to get by me."

"He plays, or I quit," Earl said.

"Forget it," Mark Anthony said. "I've got things to do, anyway."

"All right, all right. Four Eyes can work the outfield," Brian said, scowling at Mark Anthony. "And you'd better not let anything get by you, Four Eyes."

"I won't," Mark Anthony promised.

"You'd better not."

Mark Anthony picked up a glove and walked out to the outfield. He knew he wouldn't be there if it weren't for Earl. Earl was a hot-shot catcher. Brian would let Mrs. Prescott play outfield to get Earl as a catcher.

Brian and Earl had a short conference, and then Brian motioned Mark Anthony to center field, right behind the pitcher. Two little guys—Shorty Travis and Johnny McGee—were playing right and left field. Neither of them was known for speed, having very short legs, so Mark Anthony knew he'd have a lot of ground to cover.

It was hot in the outfield, and dusty. Sweat ran down Mark Anthony's face and neck. Little dust devils swirled around him and left a gritty feeling in his mouth and a scratchy sensation in his eyes. He blinked repeatedly to keep them clear.

The teams were pretty evenly matched, and no one on either team was a great hitter. The innings marched by uneventfully: 1–0; 1–1; 3–1; 3–2; 3–4; 4–4; 5–4; 5–5. Mark Anthony kept his eyes on the ball every minute. His head ached from the concentration.

The sun was getting lower, and it was getting harder to see the ball. He wished he'd brought his clip-on dark glasses.

It was the bottom of the ninth. The other team was up to bat, with two men out, two on base, and a fairly good hitter, Steven Smith, at the plate. Mark Anthony could hardly see Steven, against the glare of the lowering sun. He shifted his position several times, uneasy, trying to find a spot from which he could see Steven and the ball more clearly. The score was still 5–5. Two strikes. One more strike would do it. The next two batters after Steven weren't much better than Mark Anthony was.

There was a sharp crack and a yell. The ball had been hit hard, but he couldn't see it. Now he saw it—flashing toward him—high. He jumped, stretching every muscle, reaching, straining, and heard the ball whistle past his glove, about an inch to the left. A home run. Three men in. 8–5. He'd blown it.

He went after the ball and threw it in, grateful for the noisy celebration of the other team. If his team was saying anything to him, he couldn't hear it. He did notice that even Earl wouldn't look at him.

The game was over. Mark Anthony turned his glove in, and went after his books and jacket. Greg said, "Great going, Mark Anthony," and Brian said, "That's the last time you play outfield for me, kid." He couldn't blame them. He headed for home.

Earl caught up with him. "Hey! Wait up! Everyone makes mistakes. They're not so great themselves."

"Face it, Earl. I can't catch, I can't run without falling over my own big feet, I can't pitch and I can't hit. Who'd want me on their team? The harder I try, the worse I get, and you know it."

"Aw, come on, Mark Anthony. It's not that bad."

"Yes, it is. See you tomorrow, Earl."

He walked home alone. It was a long walk, if you were hot, and tired, and thirsty. But he was kind of glad not to have to talk to anyone, for a while.

His sister, Georgette, and some of her friends were in the playroom when he got home. He could hear them laughing and talking. All his good stuff was in there—

5

in the old toy chest or on the shelves. He wandered out to the kitchen.

His mother was starting supper. She reminded him of that Indian goddess with eight arms, at times like this. Reaching, pouring, stirring, measuring. For a small person, she covered a lot of ground fast. During the day, she worked in an office, with statistics and figures. She was very good at it. She was also a very good cook, which was more to the point as far as Mark Anthony was concerned.

He took a couple of cookies and a glass of milk.

"How long are they going to be in there, Ma?"

"I don't know, dear. Why?"

"Oh, I just need some stuff."

"Well, go on in and get it—and tell them there are cookies here, and some milk, if they'd like some. Dinner won't be ready for an hour and a half."

The girls emptied out of the playroom like water down a drain. Mark Anthony went over to the storage shelves, where he kept some of his Indian things and rocks and shells in shoe boxes. Everything was jumbled up together and wedged in tight. Everyone in the family stored stuff there. He pulled out a couple of shoe boxes, but they weren't the right ones. His boxes were probably under something else.

He thought about the ball game. Boy, just once he'd like to hit a home run with the bases loaded. He sighed, and put back another shoe box full of his father's old wristwatch bands and buttons.

He walked over to the toy chest and lifted the lid. Old Airman Jack was in there, somewhere, and all the equipment that went with him. Years ago—when Mark Anthony had been seven or eight—he'd spent whole days playing with Airman Jack and his sidekick, Charlie Wings. Once in a while, when he felt low, he still liked to get the old things out and set them up.

He pulled them out, one by one, from under Georgette's old Noah's Ark set. As he collected them, he stuffed them into the front of his flannel shirt. He had almost everything when he heard footsteps coming.

He grabbed the rest of his stuff and slammed the chest lid down.

Doris came around the corner. Big-mouth Doris.

"Hi, there, Mark Anthony. What have you got?"

"Just some of my stuff."

"Like what? Why are you hiding it?"

"You want to let me past, Doris?"

He tried to ease by her as she stood in the doorway. It wasn't easy, with all that equipment in his shirt. Then, to his horror, he felt something begin to slip and slide, and fall. A parachute kit bounced on the linoleum at his feet. Then, an anti-aircraft gun, and a tank, and Airman Jack. Everything was going, even though he was clutching it all frantically . . . Charlie Wings, a machine gun, and then—oh no!—a rubbery monkey and a little blue giraffe from the Noah's Ark. They must have gotten caught up on something when he heard footsteps coming.

Doris pointed at the pile of toys at his feet. "Oh, look at that. Little Mark Anthony's playing with a monkey and a teeny tiny blue giraffe."

7

Mark Anthony wanted to hit her. Right in the mouth. Anything to shut her up. But he knew that was out of the question. He just stepped over the toys and walked down the hall and out the front door. As it slammed to, behind him, he could hear the girls.

"Mark Anthony's playing with a little blue giraffe. Sweet little Mark Anthony."

He didn't think he would ever go home again.

His mother was still in the kitchen, cleaning up after supper, when he walked in.

"Where have you been, dear? I've been so worried."

"I'm sorry, Ma. Just walking." Mark Anthony got out the ingredients for a filling sandwich. "Ma, I need a place of my own to put things in."

"You've got all that space in the playroom."

"Come on, Ma, every time I want something, Georgette and her nutty friends are holed up in there. You saw what happened this afternoon."

His mother sighed. "Now, Mark Anthony, Georgette and her friends are just at that stage where they're not sure how they feel about boys. They'll grow out of it, eventually."

"I don't care about eventually. Tomorrow morning, that big-mouth Doris will be spreading the word around that I was playing with Georgette's Noah's Ark animals." Mark Anthony sat down at the table. "I don't need that. I'm not exactly popular at that school as it is."

His mother dried her hands on her apron and sat down across from him. "You had a bad day?"

Mark Anthony shrugged.

"I'll speak to Georgette. Maybe she can ask Doris to restrain herself."

"That won't do any good. Don't do that, Ma, please. I just need my own space, for my old stuff and my collections and my books."

"Well, if it will help . . ."

"How about Grandma Hooper's old dresser? We could move it up from the basement to the hall. It could be just mine. There are ten drawers in it—plenty of room. No one's using it."

Mrs. Crowder nodded slowly. "That's a good idea. I'm sure Grandma would want you to have it. I'll have your father move it up tonight, before he goes to bed."

"Thanks, Ma. Thanks a lot."

Mrs. Crowder called to him as he left the kitchen. "But nothing alive in there, Mark Anthony. You hear me? Nothing alive."

Uncle Edward was in his room. Mark Anthony could tell because the aroma of his cigar crept under his bedroom door and filled the hallway outside his room.

"Uncle Edward?"

"Come in, my boy. Come in."

Uncle Edward was a great big man. He had a very large, white and yellow moustache. His hair was thinning and silvery white, but his voice was strong, and deep. He spoke with gestures, like an old-fashioned actor, which was understandable because he had once been the best barker on the boardwalk at Atlantic City, and toured with a road company in the off-season.

Mark Anthony loved to talk with Uncle Edward. He always made a person feel listened to. When you were conversing with Uncle Edward, you were doing something. He used uncommon words, and rolled them out into the air proudly, and loaded them with meaning. Even listening to him was an event, a happening, particularly when he felt strongly about something. Actually, Uncle Edward felt strongly about everything. He was not a wishy-washy person.

"I see that the slings and arrows of outrageous fortune have pierced your soul again," he said, brushing newspapers off the bed so Mark Anthony could sit down.

"Yes, sir."

"Would you care to tell me about it, or do you prefer not to relive the more painful moments?"

"It's the same old stuff—this time it's Prescott and softball."

"I see."

" 'Nice and tall,' and 'Four Eyes.' "

"Ah, yes."

"It's getting so I hate to go to school."

Uncle Edward nodded. "Understandable. Indeed—inevitable."

"I tried. I really tried, but that ball got past me, and the other team won."

"Hmmmm." Uncle Edward stroked his moustache and stared down at the little oval braided rug beside his bed. The clock on his bureau ticked loudly, solemnly, on, while he stroked and thought. Finally, he raised his head.

"Mark Anthony, do you relish playing softball? Do you do it for pleasure?"

"It's OK."

"But there are other pastimes that nourish your spirit more fully?"

"Sure. Like reading, and collecting Indian stuff, and fishing."

"Then why do you do it?"

"Because the other kids do it."

"But, if you would rather be doing something else . . ."

"Look, Uncle Edward, I don't always want to be doing my own thing—alone. It gets awful lonely, if you want to know."

"Ah, yes. I do know."

Suddenly, Mark Anthony remembered that Aunt Betsy had died less than a year ago.

"I'm sorry. I didn't think."

"Of course, my boy. It's all right. Now, back to our problem."

"I try to do the things they like to do so they'll like me."

"But it isn't working."

"Well, what will work?"

Uncle Edward sighed. "I don't know." Then he drew himself up and said loudly, "I'm not admitting defeat, you understand. We are temporarily stalemated, you and I. We will, of course, find a satisfactory solution and implement it."

Mark Anthony didn't want to spread the gloom any more than he had already. "Sure, Uncle Edward. Thanks for listening."

"Have you done your words today?"

"Not yet. I'll pick them out as I go to bed."

"Good idea. May I suggest *bibulous, bigamy, bilge*

11

*water, billet-doux,* and *bigot?"* He winked at Mark Anthony. "They are all close together, interesting, and related in some way to human nature."

Shortly after Uncle Edward had come to live with the Crowders, being freshly widowed and Mrs. Crowder's only surviving elderly relative, Mark Anthony had been forced to buy a small dictionary so he could understand Uncle Edward. A month or so later, Uncle Edward had talked him into memorizing and using five new words every day. At first, he had done it just to please Uncle Edward, but lately, it had become interesting in its own right, and now he was constantly on the lookout for words which Uncle Edward might not know, or words he could use on Georgette which would leave her uncertain as to whether she had been insulted or complimented.

Naturally, he kept this ever increasing store of satisfying, fascinating, mouth-filling words hidden. At school, he was constantly on guard—carefully restricting himself to short, common words, and weeding out anything ornate or unusual. It made for very slow talking sometimes, but Mark Anthony knew it was the wise thing to do. All he needed, at this point, was for the guys to think he was trying to put on the dog. That would finish him. The big thing was to maintain a very low profile—use short, regular words, and stoop as much as possible.

He went into his room and sat down. On the bed. The only chair in the room was one of those wooden folding chairs you find in church basements. His room was one-third of a regular-sized room. When Uncle Edward had arrived, and his big brother Wellington had come home from college, his father had to partition one room to make three bedrooms. He and Georgette and Wellington were all packed in, now, side by side, in three skinny little rooms that would have made good closets. Uncle Edward had gotten Georgette's old room across the hall. It was great—having Wellington back and Uncle Edward there, and Mark Anthony didn't complain, but now he had a room to sleep in, and that was about all.

His father opened the door. Straight arm. Never a knock, or a request to enter. No. Just *zap!* and there he was. That was another thing that bothered Mark Anthony. He might as well have an Open House sign over his door, and a Do Come In doormat.

His mother once told Mark Anthony that his father did this because he was high-strung. and because all the doors in the athletic building at the college where he was a coach opened that way. After a few months of this kind of treatment, so did all the doors in the Crowder house.

"Your mother's been after me to move that old dresser upstairs."

"Yes, Dad. I really need a place to put my things."

"Your stuff is all over the house already."

"That's just what I mean."

"You've got to have this?"

"It would really help."

"All right. Let's get it over with. Come on."

They brought the dresser up and set it up in the hall. It took up a lot of space, but you could get by it if you turned sideways—unless the drawers were open.

13

"This thing is a hazard to life and limb," his father said. "What if there were a fire, and we all had to get out quickly?"

"We'd go out our bedroom windows, dear, and step right down onto the ground," Mrs. Crowder said.

"We'd better keep a light on it," his father grumbled. "We'll all be running right into it in the dark on the way to the bathroom."

"I'll bring up Georgette's little night-light from the basement. It'll look very nice," his mother said.

"What do we need this here for anyway? He's got a room of his own."

"I have to step out into the hall to make his bed," Mark Anthony's mother said crisply. "He needs more space. We'll all adjust beautifully, I'm sure."

When his mother used that tone, and talked about all of them adjusting, it meant that she was drawing a line and daring someone else to step over it.

"All these kids have too much stuff anyway," his father said, and stumped off to bed.

# CHAPTER 2

He got up wishing it was Saturday already. No school. He checked his forehead for fever. It was hard to tell on yourself, but he didn't think he had any. He looked in the bathroom mirror at his throat. Pale pink. Healthy. It was no good saying he felt sick to his stomach, which was true. His father would just say, "Eat something and go to school. You'll feel better."

He walked up the long flight of steps to the school with a churning, ready-to-heave-at-any-moment stomach. It was almost a relief when he ran into Brian and Arnold

Janssen in the hallway right away, and they let him have it.

"Well, here comes the famous baseball player—Butterfingers Crowder."

"Hey, Butterfingers, you play for the other team next time, you hear?"

Mark Anthony kept on walking. Arnold grabbed at his sleeve, missed, and ran after him.

"Hey—Baby Ruth, when are you going to learn how to catch a ball?"

His voice carried over the shuffling and chatter of the kids in the corridor. The noise around them died down a little. Everyone was watching and listening, waiting to see what Mark Anthony would do.

He felt his face burn. "Look, it was just a game, Arnold. You've let balls get past you."

"You could have caught that one, easy."

"I tried."

"No, you didn't. You just reached up like . . . you were dancing." Arnold stretched out his arms for an instant, like a ballet dancer. An appreciative ripple of giggles ran around the circle of kids around them.

"Do you want a fight?" Mark Anthony asked. "Is that what you want?"

"You take your glasses off first. I can't hit a guy with glasses on."

"I can't see without them. I need them. Don't worry about me, Arnold. They've been tempered. They won't break easy."

"We're not supposed to fight in the corridors. You're trying to get me in trouble."

"I'll be in trouble, too." For a minute, Arnold hesitated, and Mark Anthony hoped he was going to back down. But he didn't. Mark Anthony watched as he put his lunch and books down near the wall. Arnold was a squat, beefy kid, with a build like a bulldozer. He had long arms, and he swaggered when he walked. Now, he straightened up and rolled up his sleeves. Mark Anthony put his own things down.

"This is it," he thought. "He's going to kill me." He moved in closer to Arnold, fists up.

Arnold squinted down the corridor over Mark Anthony's shoulder.

"Cool it, you creep. A teacher's coming."

As Mark Anthony turned, Arnold's fist caught him right under the rib cage, and drove every bit of air out of his body. He doubled up, struggling to get his breath, making long, horrible, gasping sounds. The other kids in the corridor backed away from him, leaving him the center of a tight little circle. He heard someone say, "Go get a teacher."

Finally, he managed to inhale a little air, and then a little more. The pain in his chest eased, and the mist over his sight cleared.

"Are you all right, Mark Anthony?"

He looked up. Mr. Dobbs. Science and track.

He nodded, not daring to try to talk yet.

"What happened here?" Mr. Dobbs asked, looking around the circle.

No one answered. The other kids started to drift away, and the circle melted into a hallway full of hurrying kids.

Mr. Dobbs bent down. "Will you be OK?"

"Yes, sir."

"All right. If you feel sick later, better stop in at the nurse's office."

"Yes, sir."

He picked up his stuff and walked to his first class. He had to bend over a little, still. He ached where Arnold had hit him. And it had all been for nothing. He hadn't even touched Arnold. For a second or two, remembering, he gritted his teeth. "I could kill him," he thought.

The door to the classroom closed behind him. Mrs. Prescott rapped on her desk, and the school day had started.

After the fight, the little singsong that Doris directed at him during lunch hour hardly mattered. He didn't even bother to look up.

"How're you doing, Mark Anthony? Got your little blue giraffe with you today?"

Unable to get a rise out of him, she turned to her friends. "Mark Anthony plays with little toy animals. Would you believe it?"

Her friends giggled nervously, uncertainly. She walked away.

Earl came over and sat down beside him. He opened up his lunch bag. "That Doris is a pain. What've you got?"

"Bologna. Again. And brownies. Want one?"

"Sure." Earl accepted one of Mark Anthony's brownies and took a bite, slowly and thoughtfully. "Your Ma sure makes good brownies. You want to trade my sandwich for the other brownie?"

"No." Mark Anthony thought it over and changed

his mind. "You can have half of it. Keep your sand-wich."

"Gee, thanks. What are you doing this weekend?"

"I'm going to get all my Indian stuff out and organize it. I'm setting everything up in one spot. Ma let me have a big, old dresser for my collections."

"It sounds neat. Can I come over in the afternoon and see the Indian things?"

"Sure."

"OK. I'll see you about two."

"Hey, that's terrific! You'll really like it, Earl. I got some good things. I collected most of them right here in town, too, in the woods and along Bowditch Creek."

"How come you never showed them to me before?"

"I didn't know you liked Indian things."

"Man, everyone likes Indian things."

The bell rang, and he had only two more hours to go to the end of the school day—a Friday school day.

Uncle Edward was in his room when Mark Anthony came home. Cigar smoke in the hallway, and light under the door.

"Uncle Edward?"

"Ah, yes—it is the ruddy stripling."

"May I come in?"

"You'd better. It's difficult to talk through the door like this."

Uncle Edward was lying on the bed, with three pillows under his head and a book on his chest. *Webster's Unabridged Dictionary* supported his elbow, and an ashtray the size of a soup bowl rested on his nightstand. Cigar smoke spiraled up from deep inside it.

"How goes it, Mark Anthony?"

"Lousy."

"Bad word. Expressive, but too general. Try another one."

Mark Anthony was in no mood for word games. "I had a fight with Arnold—only it wasn't a fight. It only lasted for one punch. He got me right in the bread basket."

"Knocked the wind out of you, did he?"

"Did he ever!"

"Are you all right, my boy?"

"I'm healthy, if that's what you mean, but I'm not all right."

Uncle Edward nodded. "This Arnold—is he the school bully?

"I don't know if you could say that. He's just not afraid of anything or anyone. He walks around like he's in charge of the whole world. Everyone says, 'Yes, Arnold,' and, 'Sure, Arnold,' and if he doesn't like you, you've had it."

"Is he bigger than everyone else?"

Mark Anthony frowned. "No. Actually, he's kind of short. Short and square. Like a gorilla, if you know what I mean."

"Indeed I do. Actually, of course, gorillas are much maligned, being very peaceful, amiable—even affectionate—creatures. But the simile is apt. There is a mental picture conveyed. . . ."

"Uncle Edward."

"Yes. Well, now, first of all, I think you should reflect on Arnold's height. I find that interesting. Second, we must bear in mind the biblical injunction," Uncle Edward stood up and raised one arm heavenward. " 'Vengeance is mine; I will repay, saith the Lord.' "

Mark Anthony stirred restlessly.

"Thirdly," Uncle Edward said, sitting down again, "while we wait for divine intervention. we must take prudent action. Such as a course in karate." He shook his finger in Mark Anthony's face. "I am against violence, you understand, whether it's directed against you or against Arnold, but merely the knowledge that you are expertly prepared to defend yourself might serve as a deterrent. If not, at least he won't find you an easy mark. No pun intended."

Mark Anthony shook his head. "Where am I going to get the money for that?"

Uncle Edward said sadly, "Finances have never been one of my strong points. When it comes to managing money, my boy, I am a weak reed."

"Maybe I can earn the money this summer."

"That's possible. In fact, I think it's our best hope, so far. Doing what?"

"I don't know. I'll have to think about it."

"Do. And while you give that some thought, it may help to remember that people like Arnold frequently have a great deal of trouble coping with adult life, after they leave school."

"Uncle Edward, if I don't find some way to slow Arnold down, I may not reach adult life."

"Don't be pessimistic. It takes all the starch out of you." Uncle Edward stood up, shoved his feet into his slippers, and shuffled to the door. In the doorway, he turned back to look at Mark Anthony. "Hold the thought that you will find the money, will take the lessons, and, if necessary, will beat the stuffing out of Arnold," and waving his cigar cheerily at Mark Anthony, he disappeared around the corner.

"Shuffling off to Buffalo," Mark Anthony thought gloomily, and headed for his room.

Friday night after supper, Mark Anthony got to work on the dresser. He scrubbed it, waxed it, and polished it till it glowed. Then he started combing through shelves, drawers, pockets and shoe boxes to gather together the bits and pieces of his collections. It took all evening.

When he was finished, he was astonished at the variety and value of his own possessions. He went to bed tired but happy. Saturday he would arrange it all and show it off to Earl.

He was busy labeling and grouping arrowheads when Earl called, around ten, Saturday morning.

"What's up?" Mark Anthony asked. "You're still coming, aren't you?"

"Oh, I'm coming, all right. The thing is, I wondered if I could bring someone. Actually, two people."

"Who?"

There was a short silence. "Arnold and Brian."

"Are you kidding? Don't be silly, Earl. Knock it off." Privately, Mark Anthony thought it was not all that funny for Earl to call up and ask if he could bring the guy who had floored him the day before.

"I'm not kidding. They really want to come."

"Why?"

"To see your Indian stuff."

22

"Sure. If I'd believe that, I'd believe anything. Quit fooling around, Earl. I've got to get back to work."

"Look, Mark Anthony, can't I bring them along?"

"Just give me one good reason."

"I told you—everyone likes Indian things."

Mark Anthony felt a pleasant little thrill of pride. He had something the other kids wanted to see.

"OK. They can come, I guess."

"Thanks. That's great. We'll be there about two."

Mark Anthony hung up. He hadn't wanted to turn Earl down. If he had, maybe even Earl wouldn't have come. Besides, it sounded as if Brian and Arnold were really interested in seeing his Indian collection. Maybe they collected arrowheads and spearpoints, too.

He went back to the hall and stood there, looking down at his collections. All of a sudden, the displays looked skimpy. Especially the Indian things. Maybe he shouldn't have made such a big deal out of it.

He finished the labeling—where, when and how he'd found each arrowhead, spearpoint or tool—and then he worked on his rocks and minerals, as a sort of backup attraction. He was just getting going on his shells when his mother called him for lunch.

Last night, this stuff had looked like a million dollars to him. Now, with Brian and Arnold and Earl due in an hour or so, it looked like a lot of nothing.

# CHAPTER 3

They arrived right at two o'clock, on their bicycles. He heard them coming and ran to the front door. He was nervous. When he grabbed the doorknob, his hands were so sweaty, they slipped. Part of him wanted them to be so impressed by his collection that they would like him more. The other part of him didn't even want to let them come in, particularly Arnold.

"Hey, Mark Anthony, I hear you got some good Indian things here." Brian looked really interested.

Arnold didn't say anything.

Mark Anthony shrugged. "I like to collect stuff like that." He opened the screen door slightly, as they came up the steps onto the porch.

Earl flitted around in the background while Arnold and Brian leaned their bikes against the porch railing. Then he followed them into the front hall. It made Mark Anthony mad to see him so anxious. He grabbed Earl's arm and pulled him along the hall, ahead of the others.

"Come on, Earl—the Indian things are down here."

"You say you found all this stuff around here?" Arnold sounded as though he could hardly believe it. Mark Anthony felt another tingle of pride run through him.

"Yes. I found the first arrowheads in the root hole where a big tree had blown down, and then I found one at the entrance to a woodchuck's burrow, and three of those spearpoints in Bowditch Creek, when it was real low. The rest I found digging for worms, or under rocks—when I was collecting rocks and minerals—or just lying on the ground, under leaves and stuff."

Mark Anthony opened another drawer. "The beadwork came from a reservation. My father brought it home from a trip. The hatchet blade was dug up in Massachusetts. My brother went to college there."

"Gee," Earl said, "this is really neat. I never knew there was anything like this around." He picked up a small white "bird-point" in his hand and looked at it closely, testing its sharpness against his palm.

"Where'd you find that?" Arnold demanded.

"I got that digging for worms, in Eberhart's woods."

"It's funny," Arnold said to Brian. "I've fooled around those woods a million times. I never saw one of these," and he picked up a spearhead.

"Maybe you didn't look in the right places," Brian said.

Earl put the bird point down and picked up a quartz crystal from the rock collection. "Hey, fellows, look at this."

"You find that in Eberhart's woods, too?" Brian asked. There was a nasty tone to his voice.

"Are you saying you don't believe me?" Mark Anthony asked. He could feel his face burning red and hot.

"No, man. We're just saying it's funny how no one else ever found things like these along the creek or in the woods before. Then you come along, and there's Indian stuff all over," Brian said.

"You know," Arnold said thoughtfully, "I saw arrowheads just like these in a store, once. They were real cheap. I should have gotten some."

"Where was the store?" Brian asked. "In Eberhart's woods?"

"Hey, fellows," Earl said, "look at this abalone shell. It's from California."

"Listen, Brian," Mark Anthony said, "I found all that stuff just where I said I found it. It was there all the time. I could take you out there right now and show you where I found it."

"Sure you could."

Mark Anthony was conscious of his breath coming hard and fast, like he had just run the mile. "Darn right I could."

A door down the hall swung open, creaking a little. Uncle Edward came out into the hallway and noticed the boys. Mark Anthony had seen him do that double take a hundred times.

"Hello, there," he said warmly. "Who are your friends, Mark Anthony?"

Mark Anthony glared at Arnold. "This is Arnold Jansen. This is Brian Miller. You already know Earl."

Uncle Edward came closer. "Hello, boys. I'm Mr. Hooper, Mark Anthony's Uncle Edward." He stood in front of the group now, smiling benevolently down on them.

"Showing them your Indian things, are you? That's nice. It's a shame to be indoors on such a great day, though. Boys your age should be out, most of the time."

The group found themselves drifting slowly toward the front door.

"When I was your age, I had to be hog-tied to be kept indoors in the springtime. Yes, yes. I remember those days with pleasure. He glanced at Arnold. "Swinging through the trees," and winked at Mark Anthony, "running through the fields . . . busy from morning till night." They were at the front door now.

"It's been interesting meeting you—Arnold, was it?—and Brian. After you've said your good-byes, Mark Anthony, I'd like to see you and Earl in my room. There's a small errand I need run. Good-bye, now," and he ushered Brian and Arnold out onto the porch with a sweeping gesture of his left hand, nodding and smiling all the while.

The screen door slammed behind them. They walked

over to their bikes and pushed them over to the steps, and down onto the walk. Arnold turned.

"Who do you think you're kidding, creep? That stuff was all bought and paid for. Trying to be a big shot, aren't you?"

Brian nodded, and they got on their bikes and left.

"You shouldn't have come out," Mark Anthony said.

"I know," Uncle Edward said with a deep sigh.

"I'm glad he came out," Earl said with feeling.

"You were listening, weren't you?" Mark Anthony asked Uncle Edward.

"These walls are so thin," Uncle Edward said apologetically, "and I became aware that the situation was worsening. It sounded as though you might be forced to take on both Brian and Arnold in defense of your integrity. A fair fight is one thing, but human sacrifice is something else." He paused, and threw up his hands. "I concluded that I would have to intervene at some point, and that it would be easier to prevent an altercation than to break one up."

"I would have had Earl on my side."

Earl spoke up bravely. "Yuh."

Uncle Edward smiled at Earl. "True. But, while Earl is stout of heart, he is still slender of stature. His body has not yet caught up with his spirit. You boys were not outclassed, merely outweighed." He shook his head. "Brian and Arnold would have gone over you like Sherman marching through Georgia."

"Those idiots didn't believe me."

"They have closed minds. Tragic! At their age!" He turned on Earl, shaking his cigar in Earl's face. "You must never, ever, allow your mind to become closed."

Earl nodded vigorously, wide-eyed.

Mark Anthony said, "You want to look at the collections some more, Earl?"

Earl shook his head. "No. Everything's really neat, but I think I'll go home now."

"They're not going to beat you up or anything, Earl. You didn't lie to them. If they don't believe anyone, it's me."

Earl stepped out onto the porch. "See you Monday, at school."

"Sure."

Mark Anthony watched him ride away, and felt very lonely. The weekend he had looked forward to stretched out ahead of him now as something to be gotten through.

On top of everything else, Brian and Arnold hadn't been impressed by the collection—they'd figured it was phony—a collection of lies. They must think he'd sat down and made up every single label. They'd probably spread it all around school that he had tried to pull a fast one on them. This was the last time he'd show that collection to anyone, if he had anything to say about it.

He decided to go for a walk. Sometimes, walking made him feel better. Besides, if he found anything new, he'd have a place to put it now.

# CHAPTER 4

The trees were full of bird songs. Chipmunks and squirrels bounced along the tops of old stone walls. Everything smelled cool and fresh and green. He could hear Bowditch Creek from a long way off. The spring rains had left it high, and shoving at its banks.

He found his favorite spot, overlooking the creek. Moss, like a brilliant green carpet, covered rocks and tree stumps. Ferns hung out over the brook below. Sunlight and shadow dappled the soft, brown layer of last year's leaves at his feet. He sat down and watched

30

the creek for a long time, till it didn't matter anymore what anyone else said or did.

Finally, the dampness came through the seat of his blue jeans, and it was time to move on. He worked his way upstream. It was tricky going. The stream had eaten away at the clay under its banks. A solid-looking piece of ground might suddenly give way under the least little pressure and toss him into the creek. Here and there, a tall, slender tree had fallen across the creek when its root system was undermined.

He climbed out onto one of those trees and sat down, dangling his legs over the creek so his toes hung just inches above the water. A chickadee landed on the tree trunk not five feet away from him and watched him for a while.

He got up and walked back along the trunk to the point where its roots had pulled away from the bank. They looked like gnarled old hands, clawing at the air.

Below him, in the gaping root hole, he saw an irregular line of reddened rocks and blackened soil. He poked gently at the clay around the area with his pocketknife, and dislodged some of the rocks, opening up a small hole in the bank. Some of the rocks were shattered, and there were small lumps of charcoal packed in among them. He sat back on his haunches and studied the hole. This had to be an old hearth site. Very old. The Indians again. They had built at least one fire here, long ago, and the remains had been trapped and preserved under layers of clay carried down by spring floods. He scraped out a handful of rocks and rock chips and charcoal pieces, and put it all in a big square of aluminum foil. It just barely fit in his shirt pocket.

He always carried his knife and some foil with him—just in case he found something interesting.

Then he worked his way up the creek bank, going from rock to rock, just above the water, scanning the sides of the freshly exposed bank.

He was just about to give up when he saw another line of reddened rocks and black soil, and something that didn't look like a rock or a piece of tree root. He worked at it gently, scraping the damp clay away layer by layer till it lay in his hand. He couldn't believe it! It was a piece of a broken clay pot. An Indian pot. Wow! This had been one of the most exciting afternoons of his whole life, after all. He put the piece of pot in his other shirt pocket and started home. Earl would get a big kick out of this. Maybe he'd even bring him back here and show him the campfire traces. If that's what they were.

Earl's line was busy.

Mark Anthony wandered into the kitchen. His mother was cooking dinner. She glanced up, flushed and hurried looking.

"Oh, good. Mark Anthony. You can set the table for me. Dinner's almost ready."

"Sure, Ma. Hey—I found something, today—along Bowditch Creek. You'll never guess."

"I wonder if this chicken is really cooked. Last time I did it this way, it bled all over your father's plate, and he wouldn't eat it."

"It's cooked. It's all dark brown, isn't it? Did you hear what I said about Bowditch Creek?"

His mother looked up at him. "You didn't get wet, did you, dear? If you did, you go and take off your socks and put on dry ones right away. There are a lot of colds going around."

Mark Anthony took a deep breath. "Ma—will you listen, please?"

"Why not wait and tell me after dinner, dear? Everything's just about ready. Did you set the table yet?"

Mark Anthony walked into the dining room and started counting out the silverware.

The chicken was cooked, and everyone said how good it was. Desert was rhubarb pie. It always set Mark Anthony's teeth on edge, no matter how much sugar his mother added. He decided to pass it up, this time. He excused himself from the table and headed for his room. Georgette could help clear. He'd set the table.

He laid the piece of pot under the lamp on his night table, and studied it closely. It still needed a careful cleaning. He took out the aluminum-foil packet from his other pocket and labeled it. Someday, if he found someone he could really trust, who knew a lot about Indians, maybe he'd ask them about these rocks, and the pot. He got up and went out into the hall to store them safely in one of his Indian drawers. Georgette was just closing the top drawer—where he kept his smallest shells.

"What are you doing in my stuff?"

"Don't you yell at me."

"I'll yell at you whenever you get into my things. What were you doing?"

"I was just borrowing a couple of shells, for school.

We're studying the Pacific Ocean, and I told my teacher about your shells, and she said to bring some in."

"Oh, she did. Well, they're not your shells, and you can't. Put them back."

"Ma!" Georgette yelled, "Ma!"

"You can yell all you want, Georgette. You're not helping yourself to my shells."

His mother came around the corner.

"What's the matter?"

"Mrs. Reilly asked me to bring in some shells for a geography project and Mark Anthony won't let me borrow any."

"She just barged right in and helped herself—never asked or anything."

"It's for school. My teacher told me."

Mark Anthony's mother looked at him. "If it's for school, Mark Anthony, it does seem to me that you could let her borrow some."

"That's not the point, Ma. The point is, they're supposed to be mine—and she just waltzes in and takes what she wants without even asking."

"Well, of course she should ask." His mother turned to Georgette. "Let Mark Anthony see what you're borrowing."

Georgette opened her fists reluctantly.

Her mother said, "Oh, dear."

Mark Anthony felt sick to his stomach.

She had just grabbed two handfuls of the smallest, lightest shells—and in the excitement, she must have squeezed. Three of his most delicate shells were crumpled into little flakes, like crushed eggshells. Another shell had been cracked.

"Oh, Georgette," his mother said. "You should have been more careful."

"I'm sorry, Ma," Georgette said, and started to cry. His mother put her arms around her. Mark Anthony shoved by them, hard, and ran—down the hall to the front door, down the walk, and out into the dark. He didn't want to cry in front of Georgette.

It was late when he got back. He didn't want to come home, but he was getting awfully tired, and cold, and there was no place else to go. The lights were out in the living room. That meant the television set was off—and they had probably all gone to bed. The front door was still unlocked.

He was halfway through the living room when his father spoke. "Where have you been?"

Mark Anthony finally located him. He was sitting in the big wing chair in the corner, in the dark.

"I was walking."

"All evening?"

"Yes."

"Well, you just about ruined the whole damn evening for all of us. Your mother worried all evening. I finally sent her off to bed and said I'd wait up. Do you ever think of anyone else but yourself?"

"Do you know what happened?"

"Yes. I know. All this over a handful of little shells that you can replace any day in the week."

"That's not true. I'll have to order them, and they cost a lot of money—and I paid for them."

"With my money." His father's voice was like a slap, coming at him out of the dark.

Mark Anthony was silent. There wasn't any come-back to that. If his allowance was still really his father's money—not ever his own—then his father was right.

"What's the matter with you, anyway? I won't have it. If you run out of here again and stay away till this hour, I'll call the police. So help me!"

Mark Anthony still couldn't think of anything he could say that would make any difference.

"Haven't you got anything to say for yourself?" His father sounded as if he was getting even more angry. Mark Anthony began to panic. He'd better come up with something, fast, no matter what.

"I'm sorry Ma was upset."

"Now you look here. I let you put that dresser in the hall—against my better judgment—to keep your stuff in, but if it's going to be a bone of contention, it goes. Do you understand me?"

"Yes, sir."

"Now, go to bed."

Mark Anthony lay in bed, staring up at the ceiling. He wondered if it was different when you were grown-up. It must be. When he was six feet tall and weighed two hundred pounds, just let someone try and mess with his personal possessions. He'd live by himself, far away from here, and have everything fixed just the way he wanted it. And if he never saw Georgette—ever—it would be just fine with him.

There was a very light knock on his door. Then two more, close together. Uncle Edward. He didn't want to see or talk to anyone. He lay still.

The single knock came again—then two more. He got up and opened the door. Uncle Edward slipped in and closed the door softly behind him.

"Get back in bed and cover up."

"You heard?"

"Yes." Uncle Edward laid his hand on Mark Anthony's shoulder and began to slide it slowly, firmly, up and down over his back.

"Mark Anthony, have you ever heard anyone say that childhood is marvelous, enchanted . . . the best time of our lives?"

"Sure. Everyone says that."

Up and down, up and down, Uncle Edward's hand worked over the muscles in Mark Anthony's back, coaxing them to let up a little.

"Well, that's a lot of bilge water. Don't believe it. I wouldn't be a child again for a million dollars—tax free."

"But this afternoon, you said . . ."

"Of course, there were times when I was on top of the world—when everything was golden. Every child has moments . . . whole days, maybe . . . like that. And that kind of glory never comes around again—except on very rare occasions. I felt like that the day I got married, and the day I got the part of King Lear with a good company. I think a man must feel like that when his child is born."

Up and down, up and down. Mark Anthony worked down deeper into the pillow, finding the most comfortable spot.

"But being young is hard. Very hard. For every peak, there is a valley—no, a pit, full of creeping fear, or raging frustration, or black despair." Uncle Edward's voice painted the pits of fear, frustration and despair on the darkness before them.

"And you are so vulnerable when you're young, and so powerless." The words trailed away to a whisper. Then his voice rang out again, strong and confident. "Being an adult is like walking across a rolling prairie—some clouds, some sunshine, lots of open sky. There are great days, when you can see all the way to the horizon. And there are days when you can't see over the next little rise, and you're so tired, you can hardly go on—but the reins are in your hands."

He paused, and repeated, "The reins are in your hands then, and that makes all the difference, Mark Anthony. You may be frightened at times, and you may carry a heavy load—but you will be in charge of your own life." His voice rang out, filling the tiny room and vibrating through Mark Anthony's head. Mark Anthony could feel goose bumps rise all over his body, and the hairs on his arms stand up.

"It will only get better as you grow up, I promise." His voice sank to a whisper. "Until you get to be very old."

Up and down, up and down. Mark Anthony's eyes closed. Still, he had to be sure of something before he let go. "Even for me—you're sure it will really get better, Uncle Edward?"

"You have my word. Hold on for just a few more years, and you'll know what I mean. We've all been through it. Things will get better. Just hang on."

Up and down, up and down—Mark Anthony sighed deeply, and slept.

# CHAPTER 5

He woke up Sunday to the voice of the floor polisher zinging around the living room, bouncing off the wall-boards and the furniture. His father ran household equipment like he drove. God help anything that got in his way, Uncle Edward said. All this activity must mean company was coming.

Mark Anthony groaned. He rolled over and tried to go back to sleep. The minute he poked his head out his door, he'd get his marching orders. He'd be stuck with yard work, probably, or getting the screened porch ready. He didn't mind getting things tidy, or helping out, but if important company was coming, like someone from the college, his parents practically went into orbit. Everything had to be perfect. Not just clean. Super clean. He couldn't see it, himself. Not that he'd be asked. Just told.

His throat felt scratchy. He sat up. Where was this scratchy throat Friday, when he needed it? His head pounded a little in front, over his sinuses.

"Oh, God," he thought, "not sinus. Please. Not sinus again."

The pounding eased, but it didn't go away. Mark Anthony sighed. Some great Sunday this was going to be.

Breakfast was a drag. Everyone was polite, especially Georgette. She was trying—he had to admit it. She passed him the sugar for his cereal three times, and smiled at him once. When he pushed his chair back, she leaned forward quickly and whispered, "I'm going to get you some new shells, Mark Anthony."

He stood up. "Don't worry about it, Georgette." The kid got such a small allowance, it would be like taking candy from a baby.

His father cleared his throat loudly, and said, "Mark Anthony, you have something to say."

"I'm sorry I stayed out so late, Ma."

"That's all right, dear. I know you were upset." His mother reached over and patted his hand.

"It's not all right," his father said. "Now go straighten up your room. Company's coming."

Mark Anthony marched out of the room and down the hall. His head pounded, and his face felt hot and dry, as if he had a bad sunburn.

His mother came to his door in the middle of the morning. "Mark Anthony, may I come in?"

"Sure, Ma."

"I wonder if you'd like to help me with the porch."

"Where's Dad?"

"He's taken a load of trash to the dump. Then he'll get some extra ice, and stop by the fruit market."

"OK. I'll be out in a minute."

"Thank you, dear."

The porch ran along the back of the house. He could stay out there and work all day without running into anyone else. As long as he didn't make a lot of noise and call attention to himself, everything would stay copacetic. It was better to have something to do, anyway.

His mother brought him a sandwich and some iced tea for lunch. He was terribly thirsty. The tea tasted great. But he couldn't get the sandwich down. The next time his mother flashed past the doorway from the porch to the living room, he flagged her down.

"Ma, could I have some more tea—and maybe two aspirin?"

"What's the matter, Mark Anthony? Don't you feel well?"

"Sinus."

"Oh, dear. Do you have a fever?" She reached towards him—inside of the wrist out and positioned to register the temperature of his forehead. He ducked.

"No fever, Ma. Just headache."

"All right, dear."

The tea and aspirin helped a lot. By three, the porch

was ready. The Queen of England could come for tea on that porch and feel right at home. Mark Anthony slipped into the house and made it to his room without running into anyone. The whole house smelled of floor wax and lemon oil and pine disinfectant. Uncle Edward was still in his room—cigar smoke. On Sundays, he walked down to the drugstore early, to get his copy of *The New York Times*. Then he retreated back into his room for the day. If everything was peaceful, he might join the family for supper. When he thought about it, Mark Anthony figured this was Uncle Edward's way of maintaining a low profile.

He lay down on his bed and it felt good. This sinus attack was really getting him down. Maybe if he could sleep, he'd wake up feeling better.

It was getting dark when the headache woke him up. His throat burned and stung when he swallowed. The sheets scratched where they touched his skin. He got up to go to the bathroom and get some more aspirin. On his way back, he noticed the dresser. One end was piled high with men's sports jackets. His father's briefcase and his brother Wellington's tennis racket rested on the other. Wellington must be home.

Wellington was hardly ever home, except to sleep. Mark Anthony figured Wellington was like Big Foot—you didn't get to see him much, only his tracks—or his tennis rackets. He was good at tennis—and basketball—and just about everything else where you did something with a ball.

Mark Anthony stood there in the hallway, looking at the dresser for a moment. If he'd been a little kid, he might have cried, he felt so bad. He thought of moving everything somewhere else—maybe even just shoving it all onto the floor, so the shiny top he'd work so hard on would glow back up at him again. Then he shook his head and went back to his room. If he could just get rid of this headache, he'd feel a lot better.

He went back to sleep almost immediately, but it was a tough way to spend a night. When he wasn't being chased by something the size of the Empire State Building, he was falling—down elevator shafts, off bridges, into empty black space. His fingers ached from grabbing and digging in, but still he fell. It was a tremendous relief when his mother woke him up.

"Mark Anthony, it's seven-thirty. You'll miss the bus."

Mark Anthony sat up. His head hurt so much he closed his eyes quickly and lay back down. His throat felt as if he'd been swallowing hot swords.

"I can't get up, Ma."

He felt the wrist on his forehead.

"My heavens, you're running a temperature."

"Yes, ma'am."

"Well, you certainly can't go to school in this condition."

Mark Anthony slid back down under the covers, silently.

His mother went through the whole sick-child routine. She took his temperature, gave him aspirin, and spent ten minutes out in the hall in conference with Uncle Edward over his care and feeding during the day.

Georgette poked her head in the door. "I'm sorry you're sick. Can I have some more shells for school?"

He just waved his right hand at her.

His father came in and said, "You mind Uncle Edward, now. Don't give him any trouble."

Mark Anthony nodded.

"I expect this is the result of your evening ramble Saturday night."

Mark Anthony didn't respond. He was too tired and sick to argue, anyway.

"See you tonight. I hope you feel better," and his father was gone.

The rest of Monday was hazy—mostly sleeping, sweating, and going to the bathroom. Tuesday was more of the same, with a hacking cough thrown in. Wednesday, he woke up around nine in the morning to find Dr. Thorndike holding his wrist, taking his pulse.

"How do you feel, Mark Anthony?"

"Sort of fuzzy."

"I'll bet you do. Let me listen to your chest."

The stethoscope felt like an ice cube on his back. The room tilted and spun around him slowly while he breathed in and out on command. He fell asleep while Dr. Thorndike was still packing up his case.

Thursday, the cough felt like it was tearing him apart. His throat hurt, his chest ached, even the muscles in his stomach pulled painfully with every deep breath. There were more pills on his tray, and a medicine that burned all the way down to his stomach.

Friday, he really woke up, clearheaded, in the afternoon, and noticed that Uncle Edward had taken the church basement chair out and brought his own rocker into the bedroom and was sitting in it, reading.

"You've been here all the time, haven't you?"

"You know I have. I think I've developed saddle sores from sitting here rocking."

"Am I getting better?"

"Yes. For which I hourly thank the Creator."

"What'd I have?"

"You opened with sinus, followed that up with the flu, and peaked on Wednesday with a touch of pneumonia in your left lung. What a performance!"

"Wow!"

"Wow, indeed. You came very close to being hospitalized."

"Did I almost die?"

"No. Although I imagine you must have felt like it, on occasion."

Mark Anthony nodded. The effort made his head hurt again. He groaned, and coughed.

"Please, my boy, take it very easy. You are my responsibility right now, and a relapse would be awkward to explain. My position here is precarious, at best."

Mark Anthony reached out towards Uncle Edward. "Don't say that. Even kidding," and to his amazement, he felt hot tears running out of his eyes and down into his hair. He turned his face into his pillow.

Uncle Edward got up instantly and leaned over him. "I'm sorry, Mark Anthony. I was only joking. I'll be here as long as you need me, probably longer. Don't let my warped humor alarm you." He patted Mark Anthony's shoulder. "Rest. You must be exhausted from your recent struggle."

He took Mark Anthony's hand between his own hands, and sat down gently on the edge of the bed. "I'll stay here. You go to sleep," and Mark Anthony did.

Saturday, they decided to let Earl visit him for five minutes. Dr. Thorndike said it couldn't hurt, and it might help. Mark Anthony heard the doctor talking to his mother out in the hall, but he couldn't catch much of what was being said. He asked Uncle Edward, later.

"He was concerned that you got so very sick, so fast. He was wondering if there might be an underlying problem."

"Like what?"

"Like a chronic infection, or something similar. He ran tests. So far—nothing."

"So Earl can come over?"

"He may, if he can," Uncle Edward said, correcting him.

"Will you call him?"

"I would be honored."

"His number is 534-1211."

"When you have finished that eggnog, I shall call," Uncle Edward said, sitting back down.

Mark Anthony said, "I don't want the eggnog. Couldn't get it down. Honest."

"I see," Uncle Edward said thoughtfully. "Perhaps you would prefer your egg soft-boiled, with dry toast, or fried in a little grease."

Mark Anthony shuddered and drank the eggnog. It wasn't easy, but he finished it. He hoped fervently it would not come right back up. "There. Are you satisfied?"

Uncle Edward nodded and picked up the empty glass with a very satisfied smile, and went to phone.

Earl was impressed. "Boy—you've really got it made. I hear you've been real sick."

"I know."

"How do you feel now?"

"Tired. I can't do anything, but I'm always tired."

"Don't knock it. At least, you don't have to go to school."

"Anything new happen?"

Earl clammed up. Mark Anthony could see it happen. Everything Earl thought showed up simultaneously on his face. "Nothing special," he said.

"What's going on? You'd better tell me, Earl."

"Nothing important. When will you be coming back to school?"

"I don't know. Earl—there's something you're dying to tell me, but aren't. What is it?"

"I'm not supposed to excite you."

"Not knowing is exciting me."

Earl leaned forward. "At first, before they knew how sick you were, Brian and Arnold were going all around school saying how all that Indian stuff was fake, and that was why you weren't in school. They told everyone you weren't even really sick. Then, when the teacher said you might even have pneumonia, boy! did they look dumb."

"I don't even care anymore what they think. But don't you shoot your mouth off and get yourself involved, Earl, because I'm not having them over again for you or anyone else."

"Sure, sure, Mark Anthony."

"I found some more stuff, just before I got sick."

"What'd you find?"

"There's an aluminum-foil envelope and a piece of clay pot—top right-hand drawer in the dresser. Bring them in here."

Earl came back in a minute. He laid the envelope and the pot shard on the bed. "There's all Barbie doll stuff in there, too," he said.

"There is? In the drawer?" Mark Anthony started to get up, but thought better of it.

"Yeah. I guess that's Georgette's stuff, right?"

"Sure it is. Boy, is she a spoiled brat!"

"I thought that was supposed to be all your space."

"That's what I thought. You go get that doll stuff out of there and put it on her bed."

"I don't want to get into trouble."

"You won't. Go do it, now."

Mark Anthony leaned back and looked out the window. The trees on the lawn were full of tender new leaves, fluttering and glinting in the sun and wind. The sky was a deep, beautiful blue. A small bird darted from one tree to another, and disappeared among the leaves.

Suddenly, he had an idea. A really great idea. Earl came back into the room.

"Earl—when I'm well, I'm going to build a tree house—a real, big tree house."

"Hot dog!" Earl said. "Can I help?"

"Sure. We'll work on it together, and use it together."

"Oh, boy. That'll really be neat."

"It sure will. There's just one thing, Earl. You don't go blabbing this all over school, now. You promise?"

Mark Anthony's mother came to the door. "Time's up, Earl. If Mark Anthony's doing all right, maybe you could come back tomorrow?"

"OK. I'll call in the morning." Earl got up and started out.

"Remember," Mark Anthony called, "don't say anything."

"OK," Earl said.

Mark Anthony buried his face in the pillow so his mother wouldn't hear him coughing from talking too much.

Earl dropped by every day to discuss plans for their tree house and relay all the news from school. Uncle Edward sat and rocked, and kept Mark Anthony company whenever Earl wasn't there. Mark Anthony's mother and father popped in and out constantly during the early mornings and evenings. Still, Mark Anthony felt restless, and bored, and edgy.

One morning, Uncle Edward left him alone briefly, and walked down to the university library and carried home an armful of books about Indians.

"This is terrific, Uncle Edward. Thanks a lot."

"You're quite welcome, my boy." Uncle Edward sat down heavily in his rocker. "By the way, I met a young man at the library. He was quite interested in your Indian collection. I think he might like to see it."

Mark Anthony sat up. "Forget that, Uncle Edward. I'm not having anyone else over to see my collection."

"This young man is very knowledgeable. He is an archaeology major—you know what that means. He may be able to shed some light on the origins of your artifacts."

"No way. I'm not going through that again. Please don't ask me, Uncle Edward. You don't understand. These things are important to me, see, but to anyone else, they're not so great. No one else sees them."

"It's entirely up to you. If you change your mind, I'll get in touch with him for you."

"I appreciate your help—but let's leave him out of it."

"Consider him out."

They settled down to their reading.

A week later, Dr. Thorndike told Mark Anthony he was ready to go back to school.

"I'm not ready. I'll never be ready to go back to that school," Mark Anthony said to Uncle Edward.

"You've been gone quite a while, my boy. You will find yourself to be quite the conquering hero, I think. Pale, thinner, the survivor of a harrowing ordeal—an unbeatable combination."

"I don't think Arnold or Brian or the other kids in my class will be all that impressed. And if the teachers make over me, I've had it."

Uncle Edward nodded. "I see your point."

"Also, we're getting report cards pretty soon."

"Surely yours will be marked 'Incomplete.' "

"Yes. But before that, it'll be marked 'Unsatisfactory.' "

"Come now, Mark Anthony, the one thing that has never given you any trouble is your schoolwork."

"Well, lately I haven't been doing all that well."

"Really? May I ask why?"

"You know how they were making fun of me every darn time I answered correctly in class—and when tests came back, and everyone asked what everyone else got, how they would say stuff like, 'Mark Anthony's got another A. He's Mrs. Prescott's pet. All the teachers like Mark Anthony.' They just never let up. So—I sort of coasted for a while, to see if they would leave me alone."

"Did it work?"

"Not really. I began to get C's a lot, and I hardly ever answered in class. They started giving Heidi Mueller the needle, too. But they still don't like me."

"And the day of reckoning approacheth."

"You said it."

"Your father will be upset."

"Will he ever!"

Uncle Edward sighed. Mark Anthony's mother called him from the living room.

"Ma's home. I've got to go."

"Come back anytime."

Mark Anthony's mother had some packages.

"Here, dear. I got you a new pair of blue jeans and a shirt to match. To wear on your first day back. We're so glad you're all recovered and ready to return to school," and she hugged him lightly and handed him one of the bags.

"Thanks, Ma."

He opened the bag. Blue jeans. Neat. No big copper rivets. No thick leather patch on one hip in back, like everyone else wore. Neat—very neat. Too neat. And a blue and white checked shirt. The country-boy type. Except that no country boy he'd ever known would wear that shirt—it would look too much like his mother's tablecloth. There was just one chance. He'd lost some weight, being sick. Maybe they were too big.

His mother was standing there, waiting for a reaction.

"Hey, Ma. These are really neat." No lie.

"That's good, dear. Why don't you try them on now, to see how they fit?"

"Sure thing," Mark Anthony said. At the doorway, he turned and added, "I really appreciate your getting me these things, Ma . . . on your lunch hour, and all."

His mother smiled at him and bent to pick up the rest of her things.

Well, he'd been right about one thing. They were too big. His arms looked like bleached toothpicks, hanging down out of those starchy short sleeves, and the blue jeans were so big around his middle, he had to hold them on with a leather belt. But he knew they weren't so big that they'd be returned.

"Once you get some of that weight back, they'll be perfect," his mother said cheerfully.

"He's growing, anyway," his father said.

Uncle Edward said, "Gadzooks! You look like an ad for 'Send this boy to camp.' "

"I know."

"Is there anything I can do?"

"No. She probably took her whole lunch hour looking for these, and she thinks they look great."

"She loves you very much."

"I know she does."

"Haven't you ever asked her to let you pick out your own things?"

"Sure I have."

"And?"

"She says we should shop together—to be sure and get good value, and the right size—which means about two sizes too large. She thinks the things all the kids are wearing look kind of tacky."

"They do. But that's not the point, is it? Perhaps when the opportunity presents itself, I shall rush in where angels fear to tread, on your behalf. In the meantime . . ."

"I'll wear them. And I will grow into them."

"True. And after school, you can certainly make a case for wearing your older, smaller things."

"Right."

In spite of the shirt and jeans, and Mrs. Prescott's hovering over him like an angel in one of those religious paintings, the first few days of school went by fairly peacefully. Arnold, the real ringleader in any group action, pretty well ignored Mark Anthony. Mark Anthony gratefully went out of his way not to rock the boat. He studiously maintained his low profile and stayed as far away from Arnold as possible.

When three days of school had gone by, and Mark Anthony had not started running a temperature again, Dr. Thorndike said he could resume all normal activity.

To Mark Anthony, that meant work on the tree house. He and Earl lived in a constant state of suppressed excitement, as the weekend drew closer.

# CHAPTER 6

Saturday morning, they rendezvoused very early at the edge of Eberhart's woods, and began the search for the perfect tree. There were trees in the Crowder and Jones yards, but they were young, development trees, like all the others in the neighborhood. Young maples, mostly. What they needed was a great big, old oak, or broad, spreading beech.

The woods were jumping. Things were growing, blooming, spreading, singing, chirruping, climbing and dashing. Nothing was staying the same except for the rocks. Mark Anthony felt as if he might become airborne at any moment, floating and bouncing along in the shimmering sunlight like a helium-filled balloon.

Earl darted from one side of the path to the other, like a chipmunk, checking out dozens of trees, talking all the time. Mark Anthony remembered Uncle Edward's words, from the Saturday night before he got sick. This must be one of those golden times. Only now he knew it, so he could really feel it and promise himself to remember.

At last, they found it. It was a very old oak. It reminded Mark Anthony of Owl's residence in *Winnie-the-Pooh*, but he didn't say that to Earl.

Broad branches spread out all around the trunk. Any one of them would support a small tree house. If they built it so it was supported by two branches, it would be even safer. They found two branches on the far side of the tree, growing almost parallel to each other, less than six feet apart, for quite a distance. It was perfect, as if it had been designed for a tree house from the start.

Earl tied his handkerchief to one branch, to mark it, and they started home. It was settled. Now all they needed was the wood to build the tree house.

They went to Earl's house first, for lunch. His father was home. Earl brought up the subject of scrap lumber very casually, while they ate.

His father said, "Why don't you go over to Maple Drive, where they're building those new houses? They pile all their scraps in one place, so they can burn them later. Just don't take anything that isn't in a pile with a lot of scraps."

"Sure, Dad."

"Hey, you haven't finished your lunch."

"That's all I want, Dad. Come on, Mark Anthony."

"Good-bye, Mr. Jones," Mark Anthony said, and took off after Earl, who had a good start on him already.

The scrap piles were full of interesting things. Most of the pieces of wood were small, though. By carefully sifting through several piles on several lots, they got quite a pile of their own.

"How do we get it to the tree?" Earl asked, standing back and studying it.

"A wheelbarrow. I'll borrow my father's."

"Sure. That will work fine." And Earl was off again.

They worked all weekend. By Sunday evening, the tree house looked just as good as Mark Anthony had dreamed it would. Over the door, he proudly nailed a small sign:

**No Trespassing   Stay Out**
Property of
Mark Anthony Crowder & Earl Jones

The wheelbarrow had come from the Crowder's basement, along with two rusty hinges for the door and half the nails. The hammers, an old window with only one pane missing, half the nails, and a saw came from Mr. Jones's utility room.

"Did your father let you have this neat window?"

"Sure," Earl said. "He said anything to keep me busy and out of his hair while he worked on his records. He's being audited."

"What's that?"

"The government wants to know if he cheated on his income tax."

"Did he?"

"No, but he can't find half his records. He put them in a box when he was through with them, and now he can't find the box. He thinks someone may have thrown them out. It's making him tense. How about you? What'd you tell your father?"

"He was at a play-off. I called him up. He said I could borrow anything but the power tools, just to bring it all back in good shape."

"Didn't he ask what you were building?"

"No. Did yours?"

"No," Earl said.

"Well, then, no one but us knows about it." Somehow, that made the tree house even more special to Mark Anthony.

Earl frowned. "I sure would like to be able to show it off to just one other person."

"Why?"

"Oh, I don't know. Just so they could say how neat it was—or tell us what's wrong with it."

"Aw, come on, Earl. We don't need anyone else butting in."

"How about your Uncle Edward?"

Mark Anthony thought about that for a moment. "Yes. He'd be all right. And he'd come, too, if we asked him."

"Sure he would. OK. Let's ask him to come tomorrow afternoon."

"OK. I'll meet you here—right here—at the tree, at three-thirty tomorrow."

"Shake."

They shook on it, formally.

Then they picked up the tools and loaded them into the wheelbarrow and started off down the path. At the bend, they stopped and turned back. The tree house rested in the arms of the tree like a small box. The fresh, new wood looked naked, somehow, surrounded by rough, weathered bark and shining bronze leaves.

"Maybe we should paint it," Earl said.

"Right. Camouflage it. Dark brown and green, maybe."

"Right."

"It's a good house. Wait till we get it fixed up."

"You said it."

Uncle Edward was impressed. "You mean to tell me you boys did all this in one weekend? Why, it's just about perfect."

Mark Anthony said, "Would you like to climb up and go in?"

"Thank you, no. I am honored, of course, but climbing is out of the question, It's all I can do, some nights, to climb into bed."

"We're going to paint it brown and green, to camouflage it," Earl said proudly.

"A sound idea. Aesthetically very sound. It will blend in with its surroundings."

"It's perfectly safe, too," Mary Anthony said. "See how it rests on two of the biggest branches?"

"It does indeed. This tree is magnificent, isn't it? One of the tallest in these woods, I should imagine." He paused and then continued thoughtfully. "I expect the owner is very proud of it."

"The owner?" Mark Anthony asked. "What owner?"

"Every bit of land in these continental United States is owned by someone. Therefore, we must assume someone owns this tree."

"Eberhart does," Earl said. "Old man Eberhart. He lives in that big, old house on the other side of the woods. The one with all the fancy carving around the porch and the roof."

"Yes, I remember, on Peach Street. So there really is an Eberhart, who owns Eberhart's woods. Is the house a faded yellow? Three stories? Heavily encrusted with Victorian gingerbread? There is a very interesting octagonal room at the top, is there not—with windows all around?"

"That's it."

"Well," Uncle Edward said, "it might be diplomatic for you fellows to drop by someday soon, and let Mr. Eberhart know what you've accomplished in his oak tree. It's always better to bring the subject up, in a polite way, than to wait for him to find it out himself."

"He'll never find this tree house," Mark Anthony said.

"Possibly. Possibly. However, I must call your attention to this path. You used it to traverse these woods effortlessly. It would not be here if someone else had not been using it, and kept it open. I think you'd better approach Mr. Eberhart for his permission."

"All right," Mark Anthony said. "After we've painted it. I don't want anyone else noticing it."

"You'd better get busy then," Uncle Edward said. "There is a front due here Wednesday night—if the weatherman is to be believed."

"Wow, we'd better paint it tomorrow," Earl said.

"Right after school," Mark Anthony agreed.

Uncle Edward walked down the path, turned and studied the tree house. "I think you boys did a first-class piece of work here. Are you going to show this to your parents?"

"No way," Mark Anthony said. "Next thing you know, Georgette and her friends would be up there, and we'd be out."

Earl nodded. "Besides, they wouldn't be interested."

Uncle Edward shook his head. "Not true. However, I am a guest, not a member, so I must abide by your decision. I hope you change your minds about that later on." He waved good-bye and walked on around the curve in the path.

"Will he tell?" Earl asked fearfully.

"No. Not unless we say he can."

"What about Mr. Eberhart?"

"First we paint—to beat the rain. Then we worry about telling Mr. Eberhart."

"OK. You got any paint?"

"We've got a lot of old cans with a little left in them. Don't you have any brown or green?"

"No. I don't think so. Some white, maybe, and some purple, from the bathroom."

"What'll we do? We can't paint it in stripes, for corn's sake."

"Mix it all up together. It'll probably come out close to brown. I remember when I was a little kid, once, I mixed all my poster paints together, and I got a real muddy color."

"Well, it won't hurt to try it. I'll meet you here tomorrow with all the paint you can find. Bring a brush, too."

"Right. Shake."

Tuesday afternoon was hot and sticky. Mark Anthony scrounged around through the basement and found five cans with a little paint left in each of them, and one can of brush cleaner. He called his father at the college.

"Dad, can I have all those old cans of leftover paint and some of your rags?"

"I guess so. What for?"

"We're painting something. Can I borrow a brush?"

"OK, but I want it back when you're through—clean."

"Right. I found some brush cleaner."

"All right. And don't paint in the house—you hear?"

"OK, Dad."

Earl was waiting for him at the tree. He had three small cans and a brush with him.

"Is this all you could find?"

"Yes. What are we going to mix it in?"

"One of my big cans, I guess. Did your father mind you taking the stuff?"

"He's out of town. My mother was glad to get rid of it. She wanted me to keep on going and work on clearing out the whole utility room. I thought I'd had it. I told her I'd promised to meet you."

"Well, here goes."

The resulting paint mixture was a dull, neutral color—somewhere between purple, brown and gray.

"It's not very pretty," Earl said sadly.

"We don't want pretty. We want camouflaged. This will do it."

They cleaned the brushes and piled the paint pots neatly in a corner of the tree house, along with the rags and the can full of brush cleaner.

"We can paint the inside any day," Mark Anthony said. "The rain won't matter."

"Do you think this roof will leak?"

Mark Anthony looked up. Here and there he could see tiny slivers of light.

"It might. I'll get a couple of plastic trash bags and cover the roof with them. Maybe I'll put rocks on them to weigh them down."

"That'll do it," Earl said. "Then the stuff we put in here will be one hundred percent safe."

"It's coming along great, isn't it?"

"It sure is. When are you going to old man Eberhart's place?"

"Me? Why just me? You helped build—you help talk."

"OK, OK. When will we go?"

"Tomorrow, I guess—unless it rains."

"All right. If it doesn't rain, I'll come over to your house after school."

"Come anyway. We can watch TV or something."

They stopped for a moment at the edge of the woods, where Earl usually peeled off to go to his house.

"Boy!" Earl said, "if the kids at school could see that tree house, they'd go bananas."

"Well, they aren't going to see it, are they?" Mark

Anthony demanded. "This is going to be just our place, right?"

"Sure, sure. I've got to go. My mother will be getting mad if I'm late."

It worried Mark Anthony, what Earl had said. He stood there and watched Earl cut across the empty corner lot. Maybe that little sign over the tree-house door wasn't enough. Some people didn't think you meant what you said unless you shouted. A small sign sort of whispered politely.

He jogged back down the path leading into the woods till he ran out of breath and had to walk. When he reached the tree house, he found the bucket of white paint—there was a little left in the bottom—and a brush. He painted KEEP OUT in very large letters on every side of the tree house but the front. Then he put the brush and bucket back, and climbed down to study the effect.

The white paint had started to run a little, but anyone who could read would still get the point.

He started home again, his mind more at ease.

# CHAPTER 7

It was cloudy when Mark Anthony woke up Wednesday. Very cloudy. The rain was coming, after all. He hoped all the paint on the tree house had dried. The air was heavy. It felt almost thick, and hot on the skin.

The storm arrived while he was in school. It started with a black sky. The teachers had to turn the lights on in the classrooms, and everyone kept looking out the windows and saying how dark it was getting. Mark Anthony was delighted. It was one of the most exciting mornings he'd ever spent in school.

As they were getting ready to go into the cafeteria for lunch, the PA system came on.

The principal, Mr. Farnum, always started his announcements by clearing his throat and saying "Testing. One, two, three, four." Mark Anthony could never figure out what he thought he was testing. You could always hear him—clear out to the playground.

"This area has been placed on a tornado watch, starting at twelve noon and continuing until seven this evening. Teachers are asked to review their storm-alert sheets, and run through the evacuation drill procedure with their students. That is all."

Mark Anthony felt a shiver of excitement run down his back. He was pleasantly scared, and fascinated by the stormy sky outside. He heard Mrs. Prescott outlining the evacuation procedure. Her voice was higher pitched than usual, so he guessed she was a little frightened herself. But his attention was on the windows as he watched the small trees around the school tugging at their roots in a fitful wind.

He thought about the big oak in the middle of Eberhart's woods, and the little tree house in its lowest branches, and wondered if they had nailed it down firmly enough. They should have used more nails, but they hadn't wanted to hurt the tree. It was really a great old tree.

Everyone filed into the cafeteria, talking about the storm. He saw Earl, and made his way over to Earl's table.

"How about this storm?" Mark Anthony said.

"Do you think the tree house will be OK?"

"I don't know. Heck—most of the time these watches end up with just plain old thunderstorms."

"This one is awfully dark," Earl said, and looked out the window. His voice was light, and his face was kind of white. Mark Anthony realized that Earl was really scared.

"Come on, Earl—we're not going to have a tornado. They're just getting all excited about nothing."

They had just gotten back to class, when Mr. Farnum came on again. He cleared his throat.

"Testing. One, two, three, four. The Weather Bureau has just issued a tornado warning for Dorr County. Please remain calm. Do not panic. It is important, however, to monitor the sky for possible tornadoes in this area. We are advised to watch for trouble in the southwest quadrant of the sky. The teachers on that side of the building will keep us informed, and I am on my way up to the roof at this moment. I repeat—please remain calm. Everything will be all right."

Mark Anthony could feel the vibrations around him. Everyone was psyched up. Dorr County was only a short drive away from Ridgedale. He'd gone over there lots of times in the fall, to get cider with his father. Mrs. Prescott started to speak, had trouble with the first word, and started again.

"Now, children, it is important to remain calm. We will continue with our daily work. In the event of a tornado, we all know what to do. I'm sure the people on the southwest side will give us plenty of warning."

Outside, Mark Anthony could see lightning flicker over the trees near the horizon. Around the school, the air had become still. The sky was a sickly orange color, and the light coming through the windows was a murky greenish yellow. Like a bruise, he thought, a couple of days after it first shows up.

The lightning on the horizon slowly died away. But the color of the clouds over the school changed gradually to a heavy purple gray color. The air was still, except for an occasional odd little gust, coming out of nowhere and going nowhere. Mark Anthony could hardly sit in his seat. It was as if everything on earth was poised—waiting—holding its breath.

Suddenly, a tremendous sheet of lightning flashed through the air. Even with the classroom lights on, it was blinding. The kids all reacted. Some yelped, some drew in their breath sharply. Mrs. Prescott said "Oh!" very loudly, and sat down, as if she was feeling faint.

There was a single, sharp cracking sound, like a gunshot. The lightning had struck something nearby.

The thunder, coming right afterwards, was so close, so loud, Mark Anthony could feel it vibrate up through his feet, where they rested on the floor, and through his arms, which touched his desk. The lightning flashed again, and as it dimmed, all the lights in the classroom went out.

From all over the school, Mark Anthony could hear the cries and small shouts of startled children, and, more faintly, the undertone of teachers' voices, firm, controlled, penetrating. His heart pounded up in his throat. His palms were sweaty. This was no joke. Poor Earl. He must be really scared by now. Earl was frightened of thunderstorms, although he hid it pretty well, most of the time. Mark Anthony wished he could go to Earl's room and sit with him, to keep him company.

The thunder pounded down onto them as if it were trying to drive the school into the ground.

Then, from the village, he heard the volunteer fire company's siren. Sometimes lightning set it off when there wasn't a fire. But usually, hearing the siren during a storm meant something had been hit and was burning. Mark Anthony thought of their oak—"One of the tallest in these woods," Uncle Edward had said.

The siren wailed on and on. All over town, Mark Anthony knew, men were dropping their pens or paintbrushes or wrenches and racing to their cars. They would speed through the village towards the firehouse, headlights on, horns blaring. They should be there, some of them, in a minute . . . running past the rack where their hats and waterproof coats hung, snatching them as they ran, springing up onto the fire trucks, and revving up the motors. Mark Anthony planned to be a volunteer fireman when he got old enough. He dreamed about it, sometimes.

The lightning flashed almost continuously now. The thunder rolled first from one side of the school—then from the other. Some of the girls had their heads down on their desks and were crying softly. Little Shorty Travis looked sick. Sometimes Shorty threw up if he got upset. Mrs. Prescott must have noticed. She was walking towards Shorty's desk.

Some big drops of rain spattered on the windows near Mark Anthony's desk. Then the downpour started. The rain was so heavy, it cut off his view, like a curtain made of wrinkled cellophane.

Down in the village, the first truck had its own siren

going. He could hear it, in between the explosions of the thunder and the drumming of the rain. In another thirty seconds, it would be on its way, and the second would be warming up and sounding off. He wished he could be either at the fire station, climbing up on a truck, or sitting with Earl while all this was going on. He hoped Earl wouldn't get sick like Shorty had, poor kid.

Little by little, the electric storm wore itself out. By the regular dismissal time, the sky was still hanging over them, heavy and threatening, but the rain had stopped. The power was still out. Mr. Farnum came around to each class and started them out to the buses. No one was allowed to walk home today. Every walker was assigned to a bus and told to go straight home after getting off it. Mark Anthony saw Earl in the corridor, walking silently out to his bus. He looked as if he might have been crying, but it was hard to tell in the dark corridor. Poor Earl. He'd call him up as soon as he got home. Earl's mother would never let him come over with a tornado watch on.

Georgette wasn't on the bus. She must have taken the other bus and gone to the Scout meeting at Doris's house. His father's car was in the driveway. He didn't often get home during the afternoon. And there was a pickup truck, a very old one, pulled up in front of the house. Mark Anthony didn't recognize it.

His father was sitting in the wing chair.

"Mark Anthony?"

"Yes, sir?"

"This is Mr. Eberhart." And his father pointed to a small elderly man hunched up on their sofa, holding an old cap between his hands.

"Hello, Mr. Eberhart." Mark Anthony knew something was wrong. His father sounded strange. Cold, sort of, and very formal. Like he didn't even know Mark Anthony.

"Hello, young man," Mr. Eberhart said. "I have just told your father about the damage you did to my tree. Nearly burned my woods down, that's what you did. And what I want to know is, what's he going to do about it."

Mark Anthony felt as if everyone was talking to him in a foreign language.

"I didn't burn your woods down, Mr. Eberhart."

"Damn close, let me tell you. Just lucky for you we have this tornado watch on."

Mark Anthony sat down. He glanced at his father. His father's face looked like it had been carved out of rock, like those men on Mount Rushmore. He turned back to Mr. Eberhart.

"I'm sorry, but I don't know what you're talking about."

"You don't, huh? Did you and a friend of yours—an Earl Jones—build a tree house on my property?"

"Yes." Mark Anthony felt trapped, somehow. He knew he must be in real trouble, but he didn't know what . . . or why.

"Did you ask me if you could?"

"No, sir. I was going to see you this afternoon."

"You were, were you? That's convenient. It's also after the fact."

"What happened?" Mark Anthony could hardly hear himself, his voice was so low.

"What happened was that shack you built burned down. Nearly took my tree—my whole woods—with it."

"How could it?"

"Well, I'll tell you. First off, I thought the old tree had been hit by lightning, when I saw the smoke. But when we got over there, we found a pile of paint cans and rags and all, blazing away merry as dammit. If that shack hadn't been made of green lumber, and the heavens hadn't opened and dumped a load of rain on it, I'd have lost the whole kit and caboodle. Spontaneous combustion. Didn't you ever hear of spontaneous combustion?"

"Yes, sir. I've heard of it. I thought the house was too well ventilated for it to be a problem. There were little holes in the roof, and everything. I'm awfully sorry about the tree."

"Did you ever hear of trespassing?"

"Yes, sir."

"Good, because you're going to hear a lot more about it, you are. I'm posting my land, and if you so much as set foot on it—you or that Earl Jones—I'll have the law on both of you."

Mark Anthony looked at his father.

There was no answering movement of the eyes, nothing to show his father was aware of his appeal.

Mr. Eberhart stood up. "I've never had to post my land. Never wanted to. Now, you're responsible for me having to close it off. I'll be going now. I can see I'm not going to get any satisfaction, here. I'll give you twenty-four hours to get every splinter, every nail of that tree house off my property."

Mr. Eberhart turned suddenly, on Mr. Crowder. "What kind of a father are you, anyway, mister? You don't know what your own son's up to, and you don't stir yourself to make good when he does some damage, and by God, you don't even stick up for him or stand by him."

"We'll get the tree house out of there—don't worry," Mr. Crowder said.

"See that you do." And Mr. Eberhart stumped off toward the front door. Mark Anthony came to life again and followed him.

"Mr. Eberhart, I'm sorry. Honest. And I was going to see you. You can ask my uncle. This afternoon. I wouldn't have done anything to hurt that tree—that's just about the best tree in your whole woods."

Mr. Eberhart stopped and looked at him for a minute. Then he said, "I reckon you are sorry. So am I. Damn fool thing to do—leaving all that inflammable stuff around. Kids today aren't ever taught anything sensible—all about how to run a computer, but nothing about not burning your own house down. Feel sorry for all of us, I do. Lot of nonsense, not much common sense, that's what I say. I'll let myself out." And he did.

Mark Anthony turned back to the living room. His father still sat in the wing chair.

"I'm sorry I got you in trouble, Dad."

"I trusted you."

"What do you mean?"

"I left you alone, and you never told me you were building a tree house on someone else's land."

"I never really thought about it that way—till someone else pointed it out. I never thought it was that important."

"You didn't think. You never think—of anyone but yourself. You have no team spirit—it's always just I . . . I . . . I."

"That's not true."

"The volunteer fire department saw that house—with your name on it. Everyone in town will know about it by tonight."

"I didn't do anything bad. Just to build a tree house isn't bad."

"It resulted in the destruction of private property, didn't it? That Mr. Eberhart thinks you're a juvenile delinquent and I'm a delinquent parent. How could you do this to me?"

"I didn't *do* anything. I should have asked first, I should have taken the paint stuff away, but I didn't mean to hurt anything."

Mark Anthony's stomach tightened into a painful ball just under his ribs, and the first hot wave of nausea swept up into his throat. He gulped hard and said, "Excuse me," and ran towards the bathroom.

He could hear his father calling after him. "OK— duck out. But we'll talk more about this when I've cooled down. This subject is not closed yet, young man. You're going to have to rejoin the human race. Yes, sir!"

Mark Anthony hated to throw up. He always fought it till he had to give in and let it happen. He kept flushing the toilet and running the water, so no one could hear him.

When it was really all over, and the pain in his stomach had quit, he washed his face and combed his hair. He looked OK. White and kind of damp, but OK.

The house was quiet. His father must be in the den, at the southwest corner of the house—keeping an eye on the weather. His mother wouldn't be home yet, and Georgette was probably having a great time at Scouts. He made it to his bedroom without having to talk to anyone . . . or listen to anyone.

Uncle Edward waited an hour before he knocked.

"May I come in?"

"Yes."

Uncle Edward felt his way over to the bed and sat down. "It's dark as an abandoned mine in here."

"That's the way I want it."

"Your privilege. How are you feeling?"

"You heard?"

"Of course."

"Uncle Edward, is your position here really precarious?"

Uncle Edward sat on the bed, silent, for a full minute. Then he answered slowly.

"I don't know. I've never felt free to test its stability."

"That's why you wouldn't stick up for me this afternoon—if you heard?"

"Mark Anthony, right now, you and I need each other very much. That's what we might call a primary consideration. Everything else in secondary. Do you understand me, so far?"

"I think so."

"Frequently, I must decide how I can best help you on a long-term basis. The answer is usually to avoid making my position here untenable. Do you follow me?"

"I guess so."

"Therefore, to put it in the vernacular, I keep my mouth shut for five minutes so I can converse with you, later, for sixty minutes."

"I understand."

"Good. It has bothered me for some time now—what you must think of me in circumstances like those of this afternoon. However, I did not wish to add anxiety about me to your burdens. Now that you've brought it up, it's best to be candid."

Mark Anthony said, "Don't worry, Uncle Edward. I can fight my own battles. You just stay cool."

"Well, in this particular situation, there may actually be something concrete I can do for you. But it's going to take time—maybe as long as a week or more."

"What?"

"I won't say. In case it doesn't work—or I have to change my approach. But, if I do succeed, you will know immediately."

Mark Anthony reached out and touched Uncle Edward's arm. "Don't rock the boat here, will you? Don't get my father mad at you or anything, please."

"Have no fear, my boy. We understand each other perfectly, you and I. I will not, as you put it, 'rock the boat.' " He stood up. "It must be almost seven. The worst is over. Time to blow the all clear."

They took the tree house down Thursday afternoon. Mark Anthony's father was due at six—to inspect the area and make sure there was nothing left to mark where the house had been.

Mark Anthony had been dreading it—coming back to the tree. He was afraid one whole side of the tree would be burned off or scarred. He even dreamed about it. In his dreams, the whole woods had eventually gone up in flames, leaving a smoking, blackened wasteland around a newly painted tree house—still intact.

When he actually saw the oak, he felt about one hundred percent better. The corner of the tree house where the paint cans had been stored, and the window—framed in old, dry wood—had been burned out. But the damage to the tree itself was limited to a few leaves and twigs overhead, and a bit of charred bark underneath. The house itself lay on its side on the ground—crumpled, streaked and blackened. But the tree was OK.

They used the wheelbarrow and trucked it all back to the scrap heaps on Maple Drive. By six, Mark Anthony could not see a single nail or bit of painted wood anywhere near the tree.

His father took one long, silent look around, nodded, and walked back down the path. Mark Anthony fell into step a few paces behind him. They walked home without talking. His father was still plenty angry. Mark Anthony could even see it in the way he walked.

Report cards were handed out just as school closed, Friday afternoon.

Mark Anthony slid his card out of its envelope in his lap. It was kind of a shock at first . . . C's, D's, and Incompletes, in red ink, like pimples, all over. Well, no one could call him a teacher's pet with a card like this.

Arnold caught up with him in the hall. "How's it going, Mark Anthony? All A's?"

Mark Anthony thought Arnold's voice would rank right up there with chalk going the wrong way on a blackboard.

"No. Not all A's."

"So, let's see it."

Mark Anthony held his card out. Arnold's eyes widened. He handed it back.

"Boy, your father's going to be ripping." He sounded almost friendly.

"Don't I know it." Mark Anthony shoved the card back into its envelope and put it in his pocket. "I've got to get the bus."

"What'll he do to you?" Arnold kept up with him as the kids surged out to the line of buses drawn up to the curb.

"I don't know. Cut back on my allowance or something. Who knows?" Mark Anthony tried to sound casual. He swung himself up into the bus and let himself down into his seat. Arnold leaned up into the stairwell.

"See you tomorrow, kid."

Mr. Goss, the bus driver, tapped Arnold's shoulder. "You want to move on, Janssen? I'd like to close the door now, if it's all the same with you."

"Sure thing, Mr. Goss," Arnold said, and backed away.

The bus door squeaked shut, and the bus backed ponderously out into the school drive. Mark Anthony slumped in his seat. Now, all he had to do was show this card to his father . . . and his mother . . . and Uncle Edward. He groaned.

# CHAPTER 8

He went right to his room, and stayed busy all afternoon. He read some, and left his radio on good and loud, and worked on his fishing tackle, but the report card hung in the back of his mind like a dark cloud. Things might ease up a little at school now, but they were sure going to tighten up some at home, when this card had to be signed. He toyed with the idea of forgery, for a minute, but decided against it. First of all, he'd never get away with it, and boy! when that came out, he'd really be in trouble. Second, it was wrong—maybe even a crime.

Maybe the subject just wouldn't come up. Maybe the moon would fall down out of the sky. He was the last one to the dinner table.

Georgette brought it up, of course. "We got report cards, today. May I have the gravy, please?"

"Did you, dear?" his mother said, handing down the gravy boat. "Did you get yours, too, Mark Anthony?"

"Yes."

"Well, let's see them," his father said heartily. Mark Anthony thought he'd rather get the silent treatment than that hearty, team spirit ho-ho-ho, like a department store Santa Claus.

He pulled the card out of his pocket and handed it to his father.

"Shouldn't let it get all dog-eared like this," his father said. "It doesn't look neat. Doesn't look as if we took proper care of it."

He opened it.

He read it all the way down.

Then he handed it to Mark Anthony's mother.

"I don't know. You figure him out. I quit." And he got up and left the table.

His mother dropped the card on the table and stood up. She picked up his father's plate and silverware, and followed him into the hall.

"Whatever it is, Harry, why not finish your supper? We can all talk it over later, calmly."

"That card isn't going to look any better on a full stomach," his father shouted. "In fact, it makes me want to throw up."

Their voices blended and trailed away as they went into their bedroom at the end of the hall.

Georgette reached for the card. "Boy, that must be some report card."

Mark Anthony grabbed it away from her. "Leave it alone."

"Ma," Georgette yelled, "Ma!"

Uncle Edward rapped his knife handle on the table. "Eat your dinner, Georgette."

She looked up at him, startled.

"I said, eat your dinner. It'll get cold. I'll take this till your mother gets back," and he pulled the card out of Mark Anthony's hand. "You eat something, too."

Mark Anthony studied Georgette under his eyelashes once or twice. He decided that she looked just like a picture of a revolting peasant he'd seen in a book about the French Revolution.

The three of them sat there, shoving the food around on their plates. Mark Anthony's mother came back.

She sat down, and Uncle Edward handed over the card. She slipped it out and studied it silently. Then she looked up, not at Mark Anthony, but at Uncle Edward.

After a moment or two, she asked, "Did you look at it?"

"I have a rough idea."

"I see." She looked at Mark Anthony. "Your father wants to talk to you later." She sighed. "I don't know what the problem is, but I do know you've always been a good student till now, and you're still intelligent. Something is wrong, somewhere. Can't you talk about it?"

"Not right here, right now, Ma."

"All right, dear. Later." She glanced at Uncle Edward

nervously, and laughed. " 'Later' is filling up fast, isn't it?" Then she reached over and squeezed Mark Anthony's hand. "Everything will work out, somehow."

She turned to Georgette. "Let's see your card, dear."

Georgette went to get hers from her room. "She always likes to make a big production out of it," Mark Anthony thought. He pushed back his chair.

"May I be excused, Ma?"

"Yes, dear."

He went to his room to wait for the summons to the family conference. He really hated family conferences. Groups of people couldn't sit down and talk things over like two people could. In a group, someone was always yelling, and talking about seventy-five percent of the time; and someone else was always trying to say something and not getting anywhere. He lay down on the bed. "Of course," he thought, "sometimes it can be like that when just two people are discussing something." He groaned out loud.

They called him into the living room about eight-thirty. Uncle Edward got up to leave as he came in, but Mark Anthony's mother said, "Sit down, Uncle Edward, you don't have to go. We're all family."

Mark Anthony saw his father's eyebrows go up, but he didn't say anything.

Uncle Edward sat down.

Mark Anthony found a seat beside his mother. He wondered, for a moment, if this was what it was like to be on trial.

His father cleared his throat.

"Mark Anthony, you're getting further and further

out of line every day. Something's got to be done about it."

Uncle Edward stirred restlessly in his chair.

"I'm sorry about the report card."

" 'Sorry' doesn't cut any ice, mister. 'Sorry' doesn't get you into college. 'Sorry' doesn't get you a good job. 'Sorry' doesn't support a family."

"He's just a boy," Mark Anthony's mother protested.

"Oh, really? He's grown up enough to almost burn down Eberhart's woods. He's big enough to stay out till all hours 'walking' without permission or a word to anyone else. Just when do you think we should start bringing him up right?"

"We have been bringing him up right," Mark Anthony's mother said angrily. "For heaven's sake, Harry, the child hasn't killed someone."

"This 'child' has caused us to be held up to public and private ridicule. This 'child' will be in trouble with the police, next."

Georgette said, "I heard he burned a whole oak tree down."

"I did not. Just a few leaves got scorched, and a little bark burned."

"Well, that's what Patricia Reilly said, and her father should know. He's a volunteer fireman, so there."

His father banged on the coffee table.

"The point is, we've got to nip this in the bud. You have got too much time on your hands. What you'll get into this summer, God knows. The first thing is, I want you to register for the sports-camp program at the college. It'll be good for you to think of the team first."

Mark Anthony stood up. "No! I can't. I won't do it."

His father stood up also. "Why not? You're always saying you can't pitch, you can't run, you can't do this or that. Here's an opportunity to learn, from professionals. We couldn't even afford it if I didn't get a faculty discount. You'll be training right at the college. You can even ride over with me. It's a great opportunity."

"I can't do it. The kids who do that are good to begin with. I stink. It'll be awful. And with my own father working on the coaching staff. It'll be just like school, only worse. You'll see. And you'll hate it."

Mark Anthony was yelling now, but he didn't care. "You know why? Because I'll blow it. I won't be good at anything and everyone will know I'm your son."

He ran out of the room.

His father yelled after him, "You stay out till all hours and I'll call the police. You hear me?"

The front door banged to, behind him, and he was out . . . into the cool, quiet, moist darkness.

He circled the common in the village. There was a four-sided clock in the lighted tower of a church near the common, and he could keep track of the time. He figured he'd better be in by ten, or he might find himself down at the station.

His father and mother were watching television. He walked through the living room fast, but not fast enough.

His mother called him back.

"Mark Anthony, now that you've had a chance to consider, do you still refuse to go to the sports camp?"

"Yes, Ma. I'm not refusing, really, I just very strongly don't want to do it."

His father snorted.

"Well, your father feels that you must learn to be more responsible. So he—we—have decided that you will be in charge of the vegetable garden this year."

"The whole garden?"

"Damn right," his father said very low and gravelly. "By the end of the summer, sports camp will look good to you."

"You may charge the seeds and sprays and things at Billy's Hardware, and we will expect the garden to look well cared for at all times," his mother said.

"Thanks," Mark Anthony said. He was seething with anger. This was his father's idea—getting back. He'd never have time for anything else all summer.

"Don't be fresh to your mother," his father snapped.

"Harry, will you please let me handle this?" His mother turned back to Mark Anthony. "Maybe Uncle Edward will lend a hand, if you ask him."

"He's not to work that old man to death, out in the hot sun," his father said.

His mother threw her hands in the air. "I've had it, Harry. This is your son we're talking to, not Attila the Hun. Now handle this yourself, or let me do it. And Uncle Edward is not 'that old man.' "

His father said, "See the trouble you cause?" to Mark Anthony.

His mother said briskly, "Nothing of the kind. Go on to your room, Mark Anthony. Tomorrow is another day. It won't really be so bad." She caught his hand and pulled him closer to her and kissed his cheek. She smelled very nice. In his ear, she whispered, "It'll all work out, dear," and then she released him. For just a second or two, he stayed where he was, bent over her, and kissed her cheek very quickly. Then he straightened up and bolted for his room.

Uncle Edward shuffled across the hall around eleven o'clock. Mark Anthony heard him coming and yelled, "Come in," before he could knock.

Uncle Edward opened the door and winked at Mark Anthony. "I heard."

"Boy, I'm sunk."

"Not so. I think it all turned out very well, considering."

Mark Anthony sat up. "Maybe you *didn't* hear. I've got the whole vegetable garden to take care of."

"Wellington did it for four summers, and had time left over for tennis and swimming and girls."

"Wellington is a lot bigger than I am, and he knows a lot about gardening."

"You'll grow," Uncle Edward said comfortably, "and in a week, you'll be an expert on gardening."

"Uncle Edward, listen to me. I don't know anything about it. Honest. Nothing."

"I understand that. Tomorrow, we shall visit the local library and accept all the help it can extend to us. If the library fails us, we shall stop in at Bookworld. Books on gardening probably proliferate like books on cooking. Between the printed word and our ingenuity, we shall achieve horticultural brilliance."

"It'll mean slaving out there, every day, in the sun."

" 'Tote that barge, lift that bale'? Come now, Mark

Anthony, an hour a day should do it, once it's established. On the other hand, I'm sure your father would be delighted to enroll you at the college, and assume responsibility for the garden himself."

Mark Anthony slid down under the covers. "What time does the library open?"

"Nine o'clock. I will give you a shake at eight."

"I can't wait."

The library had one whole section—five shelves—on gardening. Mark Anthony and Uncle Edward went through the titles systematically, chose a dozen of the more likely ones, and retired to a big round table nearby, to browse through those twelve.

Mark Anthony found most of the books confusing and dull . . . the kind of book that could give you a headache if you read it too long. Even the pictures, which were almost all black-and-white, were boring.

Uncle Edward laid down the last of his group with a sigh.

"It beats me," he said, "why anyone would ever take up gardening if they approached it through this type of book."

"Dull?"

"Dull. And pedantic. Let us wend our weary way to Bookworld."

Bookworld had a much smaller selection of gardening books, but Mark Anthony found several with colored pictures, a text he could actually make some sense out of, and step-by-step, simplified instruction. Uncle Edward scanned each one as Mark Anthony finished with it. When they were through, Uncle Edward said, "This one."

He held up a soft-cover book called *Practical Vegetable Gardening.*

"Why that one?"

"Well, the fellow who wrote it is in all the pictures— it's his garden. He's not much to look at himself, but he grows a lovely cabbage. And look here—pages of instructions a five-year-old could follow. I vote for this one."

"It's your money, Uncle Edward."

"But your responsibility, and your time. I want you to be content with our selection."

Mark Anthony shrugged. "I'm content. I'm not going to be ecstatic, no matter what the book looks like."

"Good word. Well used. You're really making progress. Let us celebrate your verbal acuity with an ice-cream cone on the way home."

It was the first bright spot in Mark Anthony's day.

They took turns, Saturday afternoon, reading the book. Mark Anthony found himself experiencing a mild interest, now and then, to his surprise. Once or twice, a definite feeling of eagerness to get started stirred and subsided. He was intrigued by the variety of vegetables available, and their names. Lots of them had never appeared on the Crowder table. He thought it was great to call a tomato "Valiant," and he grinned when he read about an onion called "Ebenezer," and he'd never heard of spaghetti squash.

Uncle Edward was also intrigued, but cautious. "Let us be wildly successful with some standard safe bets, for the most part. We can razzle-dazzle them next year—if we're called upon to do this again next year."

"Just how big is that garden out there?"

"I haven't the faintest idea."

"Well, we'd better pace it off and find out."

"Already, you're beginning to sound professional," Uncle Edward said proudly.

Mark Anthony bent down to tie his sneakers.

"Do you still think we can do it?"

"Child's play, my boy. Absolute child's play. We will open with something exotic, quick growing and easy, to amaze and astound them . . . like these black and white radishes, perhaps. Can't fail. Then, while we have their attention, we'll follow up with several kinds of lettuce. We must get some seedlings tomorrow. And after that, they'll be so impressed they'll leave us alone, to carry on in our own way. If this fellow can do it—an earnest man, but not an outstanding one—we can do it. We may even come to enjoy it."

Mark Anthony felt this was going too far, but Uncle Edward's confidence was comforting. He let the last statement go by unchallenged. However, he did feel that something basic had been overlooked.

"Don't you think we'd better get the garden plowed first?"

Uncle Edward nodded approvingly. "In another year, you'll be putting out your own gardening book."

His father was home for supper. It was a quiet meal. Mark Anthony could hear everyone chewing. It seemed to him the chewing sounds started as a murmur and built to a deafening roar. He couldn't stand it. All he

88

could hear was chewing—and forks clacking on plates. He asked for the mustard, which he didn't need, just to break the spell.

As his father got up to leave the table, Mark Anthony asked, "Is it all right if I call Mr. Leyden to come and plow?"

His father said, "Yes. He can bill me. And I will expect you to keep records. Expenses, of course—item by item—and projects completed each week. 'Weeded the carrots' or 'sprayed the squash' or whatever. It would also be interesting to keep a record of your hours."

His mother spoke up. "We never insisted on that with Wellington, Harry. Expenses and jobs completed will be fine."

"It sounds like you don't trust me," Mark Anthony said.

His father said, "If the shoe fits . . ."

His mother cut in sharply. "That isn't it, at all. A record of expenses tells us what everything costs, Mark Anthony. And a record of jobs completed is a good idea, for your own information. If the corn is weedy on a Thursday, and you can say, 'I weeded it last Friday,' we'll all just have to accept the fact that the weeds grew more rapidly than usual." She shot a glance at his father, still standing at the other end of the table.

"Write down what you do, and what you plan to do, in a little notebook. No one else has to see it—it will just help you keep track, that's all." She smiled at him as if she hoped he'd go along with the idea, and not make waves.

He made the notebook that night, and he found an old manila envelope and wrote *Expenses* on it—for the cash register receipts, and bills, and other money records. He also called Mr. Leyden, who promised to come by Sunday afternoon, to "turn the garden over," as he put it. Mark Anthony had a mental picture of Mr. Leyden turning the garden over with one great swing, like he and his mother turned the mattresses every spring and fall.

He fell asleep rereading *Practical Vegetable Gardening*, and dreamed of squashes big as baseball bats, and melons that looked like footballs, and a scarecrow who kept ticking away like a taxi meter while Mark Anthony was working in the garden, keeping track of his hours.

The lettuce plants were such a delicate green, and so small and fragile looking, Mark Anthony thought they must be the rejects; but Mr. Roccio, the roadside-stand man, said they were just the right size to transplant. Mark Anthony bought forty-eight plants—four varieties. Then he and Uncle Edward went to Billy's Hardware and bought seed for red, black and white radishes, and several bags of fertilizer. They got back just in time to say hello to Mr. Leyden, who was plowing.

"You fellows sure are eager," he said. "What have you got there?"

"Lettuce and radishes," Mark Anthony said, spreading out the flats and seed packages.

"Lordy, aren't you going to raise anything else?"

"Of course we are," Mark Anthony said stiffly. "We are using succession planting."

"You'd better," Mr. Leyden said, and chuckled. He waved good-bye and chugged around the corner of the house.

"What does he know?" Mark Anthony said scornfully. "Our family eats a lot of lettuce."

Uncle Edward said, "True. But, in this case, we may have been a little overeager. We must proceed with restraint in the future, dear boy. You keep an eye on me, and I'll keep an eye on you. I am afraid we should both have been born Texans."

They raked the freshly turned soil till it looked like brown cornmeal, and set out all the little lettuce plants, following the advice of the Practical Vegetable Gardener—or PVG, as Uncle Edward was beginning to refer to him—to the smallest detail. Then they planted a row of radishes—one-third black, one-third white, and one-third red.

"A stunning color scheme," Uncle Edward said proudly, straightening up with difficulty.

"The tops will all be green. Only the earthworms will know about the black, white and red," Mark Anthony said.

"We'll know they're there."

"Well, let's go in for dinner," Mark Anthony said.

"You have forgotten something," Uncle Edward said, pointing to page 32 in *PVG*. "Hats. For the lettuce."

Mark Anthony folded them—little triangular toy soldiers' hats—out of newspaper, and Uncle Edward set them in place and weighted down the edges with soil. Forty-eight of them.

As he handed the last cap to Uncle Edward, Mark Anthony realized that the sun had set. It was getting dark.

"What time is it?"

"After seven," Uncle Edward said.

"After seven! You see—three hours—just to plant some radishes and lettuce. This is going to be a full-time job."

"I think it's more interesting that you didn't realize it was that late. Doesn't that tell you something?"

"Yes. It tells me that if I'm not careful, I'm going to miss meals on account of this garden."

Uncle Edward smiled. "I'll believe that when I see it. To the parapets, men!" and they marched towards the kitchen.

That night, tired and stiff to the bone, Mark Anthony got out his notebook and made his first entry.

## April 23—April 29

*April 24*—Planted too many radishes today—whole, long row, 1/3 black, 1/3 red, 1/3 white—and I found out later the blacks will have to stay there quite awhile. Haven't told Uncle Edward yet. He's really looking forward to eating a black radish. Also bought more lettuce than necessary. They looked so small—hardly a mouthful each. Planted and put little newspaper caps over each one—48!—to keep the sun and wind off them till they settle in.

*April 25*—Lettuces looked real neat this morning—like the garden was being invaded by rows of tiny soldiers wearing big hats. Should put in lots of spinach, so Georgette will *have* to eat it, and a bunch of cabbage, too.

*April 26*—Found Barbie dolls in arrowhead drawer

AGAIN. Put in bags and stored in attic for safekeeping. Will tell Georgette, later.

*April 28*—1/2 row spinach in. Uncle Edward caught on and made me stop at 1/2 row. Dozen heads of cabbage transplanted—used some of the lettuce hats. Lettuces on their own, now.

*April 29*—Planted six big pots snow peas—strings all around edges tied to dowel in middle, like a maypole. Peas will grow up strings—PVG idea. Ma will be tickled. She loves snow peas. Radishes up. At least, we think those are radishes.

## April 30—May 6

*April 30*—Had to rake whole entire garden—*millions* of little weeds, all over. Planted Swiss chard in rest of spinach row. Uncle Edward says when all else fails, Swiss chard succeeds. I say, who cares? You might as well be eating tough spinach, for corn's sake. Wellington wants two drawers for his extra clothes. If he has all that much money for clothes, why can't he buy his own dresser????? Ma made me "adjust," so Wellington's got one of my drawers, now—PLUS the top where he keeps his old tennis racket.

*May 1*—Hats off cabbages—watered them. Planted 1/2 row beets, 1/2 row carrots. Put some of the leftover radish seeds in row. PVG says to—to mark the row. How do you get the radishes out without pulling up the other stuff? PVG doesn't say.

*May 2*—Uncle Edward says he talked to Mr. Eberhart

and I can walk in the woods again if I keep my nose clean and stay out of trouble. Uncle Edward gave his personal word. Good old Uncle Edward. Got an A on social studies test. Arnold is starting in again. I knew he would. The thing is, if I have to choose between Arnold giving me the needle at school and the whole family treating me as if I had a fungus disease, I guess I can take it better from Arnold. At least I don't have to see him after school gets out every day. I wish I lived in a cave somewhere.

## May 7—May 13

*May 7*—Had to water everything. Hot and dry. Went for walk in Eberhart's woods. Didn't find anything, but I sure was glad to be able to go back. Bought one flat of Marglobe tomatoes, one flat of Valiants. That's a neat name for something—Valiant. Waiting for cloudy day to plant.

*May 8*—Mother's Day. Peas not up yet, but gave pots to Ma anyway. Pink bows on tops. She got very emotional.

*May 9*—Beets up, maybe. No carrots yet. They're slow.

*May 11*—Cloudy. Planted tomatoes. Knocked out the bottoms of paper cups and put little collars around them—keep the cutworms out. Radishes growing like crazy.

*May 13*—Had to water AGAIN. Tomatoes looking pretty sad. Made extra-big hats to cover them. Still cloudy, no rain. Cut some outer leaves off lettuce for salad. Not bad. Georgette took some shells to Scouts for crafts. Didn't ask. I took all the rest and dumped them on her bed. She can have them. There's another drawer for Wellington. Dad still mad about camp.

## May 14—May 20

*May 14*—Picked a few red radishes. They're still too skinny. White radishes must be almost ready. Weeds coming up everywhere I watered. You can't win. Spent two hours raking and hoeing. Hard to tell weeds from seeds, sometimes. I think I hoed up some Swiss chard. By accident. I really thought it was weeds, at first, and that's the truth. Uncle Edward said I should be more careful. It's hard to be all that concerned about something that tastes like Swiss chard. But—if that's what it was, then it proves the Swiss chard is coming up—was coming up. Adults have some very strange tastes. I tasted one of Ma's martinis once, and it was just like drinking pine needles or that stringy liquid soap they put in all the school washrooms.

*May 15*—Over at Eberhart's woods. Found the charcoal places again, and one more piece of pot. Put with first piece in white shoe box, under bed.

*May 18*—White radishes still not ready. Plenty of red. Cut some more lettuce leaves. We should eat more salads around here. Lettuce may be getting ahead of us soon. Planted eighteen hills of squash—six butternut, six zucchini, six Hubbard. Planted three hills muskmelons, three hills small watermelons, two hills Big Max pumpkins. Got 26 old tires from Pappy's Service Sta-

95

tion and put an old tire around each hill, as a mulch. Dad says it looks like an auto junkyard out there. The leaves will cover them. It took me four trips with the wheelbarrow to bring them all home. Carrots up. I thought they were headed the wrong way—to China.

*May 20*—The big news is BEANS. We followed along behind a state highway truck cleaning out the right-of-way along Hardscrabble Road and got twenty long, skinny saplings. Made a maypole thing out of them, like Ma's pots, only as big as a tent. Planted scarlet runner and Kentucky Wonder beans around the base of each pole. They should look really wild when they've grown up the poles and started to bloom. Scarlet runner has red flowers. Uncle Edward says it will be our pièce de résistance—in other words, our big number. We left the north side open, to get in for spraying, maybe, or picking, if we're lucky. And we hung a big, bright red college-type banner, with DOGGONE U. in white felt letters, from the top. This gardening is more fun than I thought it might be.

## May 21—May 27

*May 21*—Picked a lot of red radishes. Planted some more in same row. Very nice.

*May 23*—Got an A in math. Could not believe it. Also an A in English. Arnold "accidentally" knocked my books on floor going to lunch. Here we go again. My only hope is if Arnold moves, or gets smart suddenly, during the summer—which is not likely. He's worse now than he was before the last report card . . .

as if he thought I'd tricked him into talking to me for a while back then. Big deal.

*May 25*—Picked some white radishes. It took me a minute to psych myself up to try one. Not bad, for a radish. Uncle Edward says anyone with an open mind has to have an adventurous stomach. A person could get tired of radishes and lettuce, though. Got sunburn on back of neck that rubs on every shirt collar I own. Zucchini coming up.

*May 26*—Melons—muskmelons, that is—coming up. I love the way the earth cracks over them before they poke through—like we had had miniature earthquakes all over.

## May 28—June 3

*May 28*—Uncle Edward went through woods with me to see campfire site. We sat and talked for a couple of hours.

*May 29*—Flea beetles thick as dammit on the tomatoes, all of a sudden. Uncle Edward sprayed late in day. Cut lots of lettuce—gave some away to Earl's family.

*May 30*—A few beans are up. The ground is cracking all around every pole, so lots more are coming. Memorial Day. Went to parade in town—met Mr. Eberhart. Talked to Uncle Edward and me for half an hour just as if nothing had ever happened. Said we should try watering our Big Max pumpkins with "manure tea" every week or so. Sounds gross to me. He gave the recipe to Uncle Edward. Uncle Edward said we would get some manure and try it.

*June 1*—Georgette's birthday. Gave her a little suitcase to put her Barbie doll stuff in with a lock and everything. Hope she takes the hint. She had about eight friends over for supper. Ye gods!

*June 2*—Weeded and hoed for two hours—everything. If the vegetables grew like the weeds, we'd be all set.

*June 3*—Came home from school, saw big brown hill in back—manure. Gift from Mr. Eberhart to Uncle Edward. I never knew he had an old horse back there—and a cow and some hens. Uncle Edward says they're not productive any longer, but Mr. Eberhart keeps them for company. He must be awful lonely. Anyhow—there it was. We got to work, top-dressing with the manure, right away. Dad came home and went around slamming all the windows shut and swearing. Uncle Edward and I thought it smelled kind of nice. And it was all crumbly and dry—easy to handle. We started a big pail of manure tea, too. Took some lettuce over to Mr. Eberhart after supper. Uncle Edward asked Dad if, hypothetically speaking, I ever grew so much stuff Ma couldn't use it, could I sell it and keep the money? Dad said that would never happen, but yes. Uncle Edward came back out and said, "Shovel on more coal, Mark Anthony,"—meaning more manure.

## June 4—June 10

*June 4*—We got desperate, so I took some sample lettuce down to the vegetable stand. The guy down there, Mr. Roccio, said he'd take anything that was really fresh, and the price was right. To come back at the end of the day for the unsold stuff. Uncle Edward arranged all our surplus lettuce in a wooden box, with radishes here and there as bonuses. Then he sprinkled the box with water. It looked like a picture in a cookbook. Mr. Roccio sold every lettuce! Bought some bush bean seed, and more loose-leaf lettuce seed. Took Uncle Edward to movies with some of the lettuce money, to celebrate.

*June 5*—Rained. Heavy. Uncle Edward said it could only do us good . . . working manure down in.

*June 7*—Ground drying out—weeds coming back. Spent TWO HOURS weeding. Planted bush beans, and lettuce right behind them, so beans will shade lettuce a little. Back is killing me. Uncle Edward rubbed liniment on me. I smell like a hospital.

## June 11—June 17

*June 11*—Took some more lettuce and radishes to Mr. Roccio for weekend sales. Sold every one by nightfall. Wants more stuff.

*June 15*—Cut first Swiss chard. Uncle Edward and I opened account at bank—$5.00. We put it in both of our names, so either one could get it out without the other—which was a very good idea. That way, if I should happen to keel over from heatstroke or something, weeding, Uncle Edward could still get to our money. It could happen.

*June 17*—Last day of school. Three cheers. Report cards. 3 A's, rest B's. Plus lots of comment. Felt a little like that booby in the Bible—the prodigal son, I think.

Arnold was all over me like slither on a snake—
"What'd you get, Mark Anthony? Teacher's pet, Mark
Anthony." I figured, just let me get out of here, God, I
don't have to see his ugly face till September. But as I
climb up into the bus, he grabs my leg and pulls, and I
give him a shove, to get loose, and over he goes—PLUS
two of his buddies standing behind him. So—it was
back to the office for fighting . . . which was a new ex-
perience, and kind of neat. Everyone passing the office
looked in and kept on going, as if they were glad it was
us and not them in there. The principal bawled us all
out, as if we were a gang, for corn's sake. Arnold
looked disgusted. I had to walk home because the bus
had left without me. Uncle Edward said I got "mixed
reviews" at supper. Dad looked at my card and
grunted. Then he said, "By the way, while I certainly
do not approve of fighting, outside of the ring—you
understand?—I'm glad you're starting to stick up for
yourself." Ma was happy about the card and upset
about the fighting. She must have asked me ten times
if I was all right. Georgette looked impressed, which
doesn't happen too often. I felt kind of like a phony, to
tell the truth. It was just a real lucky shove. I didn't de-
serve all that credit.

## June 18—June 24

*June 18*—Took some Swiss chard to Mr. Roccio, arranged it with white icicle radishes. A little still unsold
by suppertime. It figures. You couldn't give it away to
me. Everyone says, "If he grows it himself, and sees it

coming up and all, he'll learn to love it." No way, I could sit there and watch it grow all day, and when I put a forkful in my mouth, it would still taste like rusty nails.

*June 19*—Got up early, went fishing. Ran out of bait and used a piece of cheese I'd brought with me for breakfast—caught a trout! He wasn't big, but a trout is a trout. Gave it to Ma to be Dad's own special dinner, in honor of Father's Day. Also gave him some shaving lotion . . . called "Super-Man". Dad said he liked it. And he ate all of his trout.

*June 20*—First beets are in. I'm going to plant more beans—the maypole sure is a sight. The green creeps up the sides every day now. I can see the difference. I water it whenever I can. Dad says it looks like a circus tent out there. Actually, with the red banner at the top, it looks more like something out of King Arthur's court. Very classy.

*June 21*—Earl came over and we watched a dumb horror movie on TV. Nothing to do in the garden today. I feel like I must have forgotten something—but even gardeners get a day off once in a while, I guess.

## June 25—July 1

*June 28*—Zucchini are in—little ones like dark green fingers. Ma says they cook up in about five minutes. Also pulled a few nice little carrots. Ma's peas are almost ready.

*June 29*—Got up very early, while it was cool, and went over to Eberhart's woods. Found small cave, going way back under hill. Entrance is all overgrown. Actually, I tripped into it, sort of by accident. Anyway, I brought out some pieces of charcoal, which could be from Indian fires, and a scraper—I think it's a scraper—for animal skins. Hid them in the shoe boxes under my bed.

*June 30*—Made up two small mixed boxes in morning, took them down to Mr. Roccio. He went crazy—little vegetables sell for more than big ones. Can you beat that! They're supposed to be more tender and tasty. The people driving by on the highway stop at his stand in droves. He was sold out by six. Mr. Roccio gave Uncle Edward a little bottle of his homemade wine. I watered for an hour this evening. The garden sure smells nice. Uncle Edward says I should consider become a farmer, but I want to be an archaeologist. That's all I've ever wanted to be, really. It's kind of an oddball thing to be, though.

## July 2—July 8

*July 4*—Our own tomatoes, peas. Got two small boxes down to Mr. Roccio. Cleaned out the garden to do it. Hope Ma doesn't ask for anything tonight. Fireworks display over the lake, if it doesn't rain—and the J.C.'s carnival. The whole family is going. I'm going to ask for potato salad, specifically, for the picnic supper—otherwise, Ma might try to scrounge up a big tossed salad. We'd have to give her radish tops and dandelion greens because everything else is down at Mr. Roccio's stand.

102

*July 5*—Hot! Great fireworks last night. Had to hoe for one hour. Uncle Edward gave up and sat on the porch drinking iced tea.

*July 6*—Still hot. Thunderstorm late in day—heavy rain. Hosed everything down afterwards, to wash all the dirt and manure off the leaves. The garden really looks neat.

*July 7*—Some of the beans have made it all the way to the top of their poles. The whole maypole is green now, and with the red banner on top, it's a sight. It looks like a tent for royalty, if you look at it with your eyes almost closed. Earl brought his dad over to see it. Mr. Jones said it was something else.

## July 9—July 15

*July 9*—Nothing for Mr. Roccio. He called to see if we could spare him a couple of boxes of stuff. I had to say no. He called back later, and asked if we were mad about something or wanted a bigger cut. Uncle Edward said we had a deal—we weren't holding him up—and went into his, "Who steals my purse steals trash . . ." bit. Everybody here is eating as if it's going out of style. Ma makes big salads every night. I don't dare say anything, in case Dad blows the whistle on our deal with Mr. Roccio. But I'm watering a lot, and we've used up the last of the manure. It's all in there, some-where. The garden practically *steams* when the sun hits it in the morning. I'm not kidding.

*July 11*—Succession planting. Carrots, beets—one row each. Bush beans and lettuce—half a row. Stiff all over when I got through. Soaked in a hot tub till I was bright red—then liniment, again.

*July 12*—Uncle Edward went over to the cave with me—but not in. Too little cave, too much Uncle Edward. He's an awful good sport. I worked the whole garden over in the afternoon—hoed every single row. Came in around supper feeling awful. Ma said I had a "touch of sun." Had to lie down all evening, and didn't even want to watch TV.

## July 16—July 22

*July 16*—Three boxes for Mr. Roccio . . . a little of everything. Uncle Edward sure does a great job. When he gets through arranging things and spraying them with water, I feel like buying them myself. Mr. Roccio happy again.

*July 18*—Back to the bank. Weeded, sprayed beans for an hour—early in the day. Discovered space inside bean tent is really neat. Cool and shady. Set up two chairs in there in afternoon. Uncle Edward and I spent a couple of hours reading. Planted more beans at base of each pole.

*July 19*—Rabbits giving us trouble. Nibbling. Just a little here, a little there, but people don't like to eat something a rabbit's been eating first. Even if you wash it. Uncle Edward and Mr. Eberhart say a chicken-wire fence will do the trick.

*July 20*—Asked Dad to go in with me on chicken wire. He said it would be cheaper to buy the vegetables. Ma said it would not. She'd go in with me on the wire, 50–50, if I put it up. I think Dad is mad at me again.

*July 21*—Georgette asked for a couple of drawers in dresser, "like Wellington's got." She's running out of space for her stuffed animals. I'd like to stuff her. Ma said she could have one drawer. Which means the whole dresser. Georgette spreads out. She's pushy because she knows she can get away with it. Pushy people are like that, boy—careful. They figure the odds, and when the odds are right, they shove.

## July 23—July 29

*July 23*—Put in chicken-wire fencing. Earl helped. Paid him a dollar an hour. He says if I've got any more jobs, call him.

*July 24*—Picked our first beans from the maypole. Ate some raw, even—pretty good. Too good. Ma says she'd like to can some. There is such a thing as being too successful for your own good. Mr. Roccio will have to wait for beans.

*July 25*—Moved an orange crate full of books out to the bean maypole and covered it with plastic to keep rain and dew off. Hot as the hinges today. Read in the afternoon. Weeded after supper. Mosquitoes are really getting to me.

*July 26*—Big thunderstorm last night. Nice and cool this morning. Have all my Indian stuff safe in shoe boxes under my bed now . . . sorted, labeled and everything. I label it by how and where and when I found it, but that's all, because I don't know the rest. I don't think it was all done by the same tribe, because the chipping and shaping aren't the same on all the points, and several different kinds of rocks were used. Uncle Edward went through it with me this afternoon. He said I should show it to that fellow at the university. NO WAY. I'm not going to be called a liar, or made fun of again, if I can help it.

## July 30—Aug. 5

*July 30*—Beans for Mr. Roccio—plus an assorted crate. He snapped a couple of beans between his fingers, and then he ate one raw. He said they would go in his "deluxe case." Uncle Edward went over to visit Mr. Eberhart this afternoon. He took some tomatoes, beans, radishes, lettuce and a bag of cookies Ma had made. We called it our "We Care" box. Mr. Eberhart and Uncle Edward are getting to be real good friends.

*Aug. 3*—The melons are ready. Man! My mouth has been watering for a month. Got one sweet little cantaloupe and one small watermelon. I ate them both—gave everyone else a tiny slice—and I never ate anything so good in all my life. Spent afternoon in maypole. Mr. Eberhart came by and sat and talked with Uncle Edward while I read. Said pumpkins were coming right along. Took off ends of vines to stop more vine growth, and picked all the little pumpkins but one off of two vines, so those two vines will concentrate on one pumpkin each. I might end up with a couple of pumpkins that weigh as much as Ma does. Went to bank. Our account is really growing.

*Aug. 4*—Uncle Edward put my old toys and stuff in the bottom of his closet. My books are all over—mostly out in the maypole. Hot sticky day—you could practically see things grow. Uncle Edward says out in Kansas, on a day like today, if you stood in a cornfield, you could *hear* the corn grow.

*Aug. 5*—Three boxes to Mr. Roccio, plus a personal melon for him. Watered for an hour after supper. Moon came out early. Saw rabbits dancing and playing on the lawn.

## Aug. 6—Aug. 12

*Aug. 6*—Mr. Eberhart came by. I could tell he was leading up to something. Sure enough, after an hour of "Isn't it hot?" and "Those are the best beans I ever ate," he got down to it. Could he see my Indian stuff? I said no. Nicely. Uncle Edward gave me the fisheye. So I said I'd bring it out—and I did. But not all of it. I never thought Uncle Edward would put the squeeze on me like that—in front of someone else. I just dumped the stuff down and left. I don't care what anyone else thinks about my stuff. I like it. I like to pick it up, and hold it, and think about the people who made it and depended on it years ago. I wonder about whether or not the "bird-points" brought down any birds for them when they were hungry. About the lady who cooked with the pot—did she have any children? If I wanted to fool around and collect this stuff, that's my business isn't it—and I wish everyone else would just leave me alone. I think Uncle Edward is so sold on Mr. Eberhart, now, that he doesn't care whether I mind or not.

*Aug. 7*—Still angry with Uncle Edward. I wish I wasn't. He's the best friend I ever had. But I can't help it. That's all over now. Every time he tries to talk with me—as if everything were OK—I get nasty or clam up. Sometimes I think, "That's like my father is," and I hate that—but I just keep on slamming doors or giving him the silent treatment.

*Aug. 8*—Four boxes to Mr. Roccio, plus a lot of stuff for Ma. Uncle Edward came by last night, after I'd gone to bed, and knocked. I didn't answer. He came in anyway. He said Mr. Eberhart had been very interested in the Indian collection, and that it had been found on his property, after all. I said that wasn't why I was mad. He said he knew—that I resented being pushed to satisfy someone else's curiosity. Then he said, "I'm sorry, Mark Anthony. I was wrong." Just like that. What could I do? I had to tell him it was all right, right? So we're friends again, and I'm glad. I feel about a thousand pounds lighter.

## Aug. 13—Aug. 19

*Aug. 13*—Three weeks and a few days till school. At night, it's already getting colder. I feel like I'm slipping back into one of those pits of despair Uncle Edward was talking about. I wish it were June again. Ma's canning like mad. Mr. Roccio will take all the beans we can send over. Between the two of them, hardly a bean on the whole maypole gets to grow to its full length. Went to the bank. I never had a lot of money of my own before. It feels real good.

*Aug. 15*—Weighed biggest pumpkin. *Ninety-eight pounds!* I couldn't believe it. Uncle Edward says it's all that manure tea. Spent afternoon in maypole with Earl and Uncle Edward, reading and talking.

*Aug. 16*—Went for walk in woods—ran into Mr. Eberhart. I knew it. I'll bet he's out there every day now, looking for Indian stuff. What can I say? It's his land, isn't it? I showed him the campfire sites. He told me a lot of stories about when he was a kid. He really likes Uncle Edward. That's one thing we agree on. As we left, he said, "You've got the touch, Mark Anthony. Been looking all day, and haven't found a thing." I felt guilty, but it made me feel good, too.

*Aug. 19*—Ma and Dad and Georgette are going to Indianapolis, tomorrow. Uncle Edward and I get to stay home. At first, Dad said I had to go; I didn't want to. They're going to stay with Uncle Julius—my father's brother—Julius Caesar Crowder. Everyone in Dad's family has a big name—Julius Caesar Crowder, Light-Horse Harry Lee Crowder, Mark Anthony Crowder, Wellington Waterloo Crowder. Georgette Sands Crowder—I mean, what are they trying to prove! If I have a son, I'm going to call him Sam. Period. Anyway, Uncle Julius is just like Dad, so they get on each other's nerves sometimes, and after a few days of doors slamming, suppers with no one speaking to anyone else, and fights over the TV set, I've had it. Besides, we can't leave the garden. Ma said I could stay. Ma looked as if she would like to stay, too.

## Aug. 20—Aug. 26

*Aug. 20*—Two weeks and a few days till school. Lots of things in the garden are slowing down. I can see it. Fall's coming. Little spaces between vines, here and there, on maypole.

*Aug. 23*—Heavy rain—windy. Covered books and things in maypole tent with extra plastic. Winter carrots, beets, squash, coming along. Lettuce beaten down a little by storm.

*Aug. 24*—Fall lettuce perking up again. Uncle Edward wants to go to university library some day soon—asked me to go along to help carry books home. His back is bothering him. I hope I haven't let him do too much in garden. Mr. Roccio wants at least one of biggest pumpkins for display. Said he'd pay me 10¢ a pound. When I told him how many pounds I was shooting for, and that they might not be good eating pumpkins, he said, "I don't care about eating, these are advertising pumpkins." Uncle Edward said to take the money and run. Way back, Georgette said she wanted one for Halloween, and I thought she would get one of the biggest, but Ma said, "Nonsense, Georgette. Two of the small ones will be fine." And that was that. Ma's really neat, sometimes.

*Aug. 26*—Everybody home again. When I asked Ma how it went, she said, "Don't ask." Dad just sort of growled.

## Aug. 27—Sept. 2

*Aug. 27*—Turned pumpkins, *very* carefully. Took two boxes of mixed produce to Mr. Roccio early in the day. Needs more if I can get it away from Ma. Went to library with Uncle Edward—met that fellow who's an archaeology major—does some assistant teaching, even. "Rodger Dodger," Uncle Edward calls him. He is so *short*—and wiry. I'll bet he doesn't weigh over one hundred and twenty pounds. Hey—not much more than one of my pumpkins! But he was really nice. Took us out for coffee. I drank mine with about three sugars and two milks—not bad. He said, "Mark Anthony, I believe we have a problem in common." I said, "Oh, yeah?" He said, "Yes—height." I guess my mouth fell open. He laughed and said, "Hey—don't you think being short has its drawbacks?" I said, "At least you don't stick out like a sore thumb, in a crowd." He said, "No, but I get stepped on a lot. Besides—the rest of them will grow, and catch up with you, but no one's going to shrink, and come down to my size." I said, "Heck, Rodger, size doesn't matter with a guy like you," and he said, "That's funny, I heard someone say just the same thing about you, Mark Anthony." Uncle Edward picked out only about four books, after all that. I sure feel bad about his back. Used to be, he'd carry home eight or ten books with no trouble.

111

*Sept. 1*—Looks like lots of stuff will be ready to be canned, and a lot left over for Mr. Roccio. One more spraying, and one more watering, and then everything out there is on its own.

*Sept. 2*—Picked and packed. Took a couple of boxes over to Mr. Roccio after supper. Ma went to bed early—tomorrow is relish, pickle, piccalilli and tomato-conserve day.

## Sept. 3—Sept. 9

*Sept. 3*—Ma was up with the sun and the birds. Everyone had to go out to McDonald's for breakfast. By noon, she must have had four different things working. It smelled great. I washed and sterilized bottles. *Hot* work.

*Sept. 4*—Mr. Roccio called—more produce. I scraped up one small boxful and took it over. Watered early, sprayed late in day. Spent afternoon in maypole. It's really something, to sit in there. The light inside is green, like you were underwater. But, if you sit in the right place, the sun will fall on your book. No one can see you unless they're standing right in the entrance. All the house noises are kind of distant, once you're inside. It's sort of restful, and hidden, and private.

*Sept. 5*—Doris, Georgette's big-mouth friend, came around. The two of them came out to the maypole and started mouthing off. Uncle Edward went inside. I stuck it out till they tried to come in. Then I said, "Georgette, beat it. You can't come in." She pushed a little. I said, "Georgette, you shove me once more and

I'll pick up a handful of this manure and dirt and rub it in your hair." And I meant it, too. She went into the house to complain to Ma, but Ma never did come out, so I guess I got away with it, this time. I stayed out there till dinner. I think I can see gaps in the vines at the top, now. It makes me feel sad to see that. I'm going to miss this old maypole. It's Labor Day—a holiday. I sure don't feel like celebrating.

*Sept. 6*—To the bank. Every time I look at the amount, I am really sort of surprised. Of course, a lot of that hundred dollars really should go to Uncle Edward. He says he won't take a penny. Ma made me go shopping for clothes with her. School tomorrow. We compromised a lot. Naturally, I had grown some more. Sometimes I think I have a glandular problem. Overheard Georgette and Wellington arguing about space in the dresser. Dad's easing up a little now that the sports camp is closed. I guess that was a constant reminder of how much I'd let him down. It's cold tonight. Cold weather means the only places I can be are in the house or in school. Pretty soon, the maypole will be getting patchy, and after that, it'll be just a matter of time till first frost—and then I'd look sort of foolish, sitting out there where everyone could see me through the bare poles.

*Sept. 7*—Got Mr. Dobbs for homeroom. Arnold and his friends are back. I wonder if there's any way someone my age could get out of going to school. Even if there was, my father wouldn't let me do it. Rodger Dodger came by tonight, to see Uncle Edward. I went across the hall, and we all sat around and talked. He really knows a lot about Indians.

113

*Sept. 10*—Hubbard squashes and pumpkins so nearly ready, I'm itching to take them in—in case something happens to them. Lots of small, winter stuff ready to be harvested anytime—beets, carrots, etc. Maypole definitely thinning out. Moved books and stuff indoors—to closets, etc. Wrote down what I did with everything. Put the paper in shoe box with pot shards.

*Sept. 11*—Rodger Dodger came by but Uncle Edward was gone—out for his paper and a walk. Took him into my room to wait. We got to talking about Indians, and he kept hinting around. And finally I ended up showing him all my stuff. He was really nice about it—said it was a surprising collection, that the area they came from should be investigated. Well, he's really keen on Uncle Edward, so what else could he say? He took a couple of things with him, back to the university, for some reason. Promised to return them real soon.

*Sept. 15*—Rodger Dodger came by and asked if he could take the rest of my Indian things for a couple of days. He was really cagey about why. It worries me, to tell the truth, but Uncle Edward says Rodger can be trusted. I guess the damage is done now, anyway. If he brings them back and says something snotty, I'll deck him—so help me. I don't care if he *is* short.

## Sept. 17—Sept. 23

*Sept. 17*—Hubbards and pumpkins harvested!! Took two pumpkins to Mr. Roccio, after we weighed them on the bathroom scale. One weighed one hundred and twenty pounds, the other one hundred and fifteen. Uncle Edward helped me load them into the wheelbarrow. I guess his back is OK now. I had to make two trips. Mr. Roccio gave me $23.50 for the pumpkins alone. He also bought six Hubbard squashes—cash on the barrelhead—at 6¢ a pound. That's $28.90, total. And another trip with the wheelbarrow. I put six Hubbard squashes in the basement. Ma says that will hold us for one winter, at least.

*Sept. 18*—Dad is in Cleveland, scouting. Rodger Dodger came by. For a minute, I panicked. He didn't have one shoe box with him. He asked me if we could walk through Eberhart's woods, to see the places where I found the stuff. I said sure. We walked all day. Rodger took a lot of notes, and poked and dug around. He's an easy guy to be with. I can see why Uncle Edward likes him. He says my stuff will be back next week, without fail, unless I'd like to leave it all with him a little longer. I didn't know what to say, so I didn't say anything. I hope he can figure that out. I want the stuff back. I'm really tired of waiting already. I miss it.

*Sept. 19*—Wow! Today has been one of the best days of my whole life. I was sitting in the maypole, feeling like just taking off. The summer's over, Arnold and Brian are back on my neck, I'm taller, my stuff is spread out all over, hidden away again, the garden's dying . . . when I looked up at the sky, through the top of the maypole, and said to myself, "If this were a tipi, that would be the smoke hole, and I'd have a little fire here, which would be neat." And then I said, "Why not, man?" and that was it. I'm going to convert the

115

maypole into a small tipi for the winter, with real Indian backrests, and a fire hole, and everything. I have enough money from the garden to pay for the materials, and the waterproofing, and the paints. I have the instructions in my books. So—I'll have my own place, even in cold weather. Only this time, it will really be my own place. I'll have Mr. Leyden turn the garden under but leave this place in the center alone. By the time the bean vines are dead, my tipi cover, and the lining, will be ready. Hardly anyone will even know it's back here. You can't see the garden from the street. Maybe Uncle Edward and Rodger Dodger will lend a hand.

*Sept. 20*—Dad still in Cleveland. Uncle Edward thought the tipi was a great idea. He's at the library today, but he said he'd help when I was ready. Went to the bank after school and drew out enough money. Some left for maybe eight karate lessons. Maybe I'll just learn the first couple of moves and the yells and see if I can psych Arnold out. Laid out all the cloth for the outer tipi and cut it out. Will do homework in the morning. Butternut squashes piling up in the cellar— must spread out on paper. Also, must dig a small, deep trench for root cellar—just to bury the winter stuff. We'll buy some straw from Mr. Eberhart to cover it up.

*Sept. 21*—Laid out lining for tipi—cut it out. Drew decorations and designs on lining and outer tipi cover. Ma helped. She really can draw. Dad in Indiana.

*Sept. 22*—Rearranged poles correctly—just to see what tipi would look like when it was done. A tipi is not a straight cone. It's sort of a tilted cone. It wasn't easy moving the poles with bearing bean vines still attached to most of them. Had to sort of coax them into place. It's going to look great. Dug fire hole. Ma nervous about fire. Had to show her the book so she'd quit worrying about me burning up. She still wanted me to put a Sterno stove in the fire hole instead. What Indians use Sterno in a tipi, for corn's sake? Dad due home Saturday. Will take some butternut squashes to Mr. Roccio, Saturday, and pick up straw from Mr. Eberhart.

*Sept. 23*—Dug root cellar—*four hours!* Found spearhead in trench I dug. Called Rodger Dodger—he said I had the knack, ought to be an archaeologist. How about that! Maybe I will be, after all. Uncle Edward had to work on my back—stiff as a board. Georgette and Wellington had an argument about the dresser. Ma yelled at both of them, which is really funny because they're both bigger than she is, now. In a way I was sad, because I used to think that was going to be sort of my private museum; but in a way, I couldn't help feeling satisfied. Arnold and Brian had a fight—with each other for a change. Uncle Edward says it must be the barometric pressure. Mr. Leyden due to plow tomorrow. Uncle Edward was right—I even got to enjoy the garden.

## Sept. 24—Sept. 30

*Sept. 25*—Well, if Sept. 19 was one of the best days of my life, Sept. 24 was one of the worst—probably the worst. Mr. Leyden came to plow in the afternoon. Dad had gotten home at lunch, so he went out to talk to Mr. Leyden. When I got home from Mr. Eberhart's, they were starting to pull up the tipi poles and shove them into the back of Mr. Leyden's pickup truck, with the poor bean vines still hanging on and everything. I ran out there, yelling for them to stop. Dad said, "We're taking this eyesore down, so Mr. Leyden can cart it away and plow." I said, "It's not an eyesore. It's still a set of bean poles, and it's going to be a tipi." Dad said, "Look at it—it's falling over already. I want it down." When I told him that was how tipis were built, he gave me one of those "Sure, Mac" looks, and said, "You don't know anything about tipis, and you don't need one. Now, we're taking this thing down." Ma heard us yelling and came out and said I had gotten everything ready to make the tipi and what would it hurt? Dad said, "You mean you knew about this? And you let him?" And Mr. Leyden said he could come back another day. Georgette came out and said everyone at school would laugh at her because she had such a weird brother, and I told her to shut up, and Dad swung at me. He missed, but I got out of there fast.

I spent a couple of hours in the woods, but then I was getting so cold I couldn't take it any longer, so I went to Mr. Eberhart's house. I figured Dad would never look there, but he'd call Earl right away. Mr. Eberhart gave me Irish coffee, which was very strong and sweet and had something else in it—brandy or whiskey, I think—and it did make me feel a lot warmer and sleepy. Then he called my house and asked for Uncle Edward, and told him that an unexpected guest had come by, and Uncle Edward caught on right away.

I didn't want him to call, but I figured I wasn't going back anyway, no matter what. So if they came to get

118

me, I'd just leave. Mr. Eberhart said I could trust Uncle Edward to do right by everyone concerned, and I knew he was right. I wanted Ma to know just enough so she wouldn't worry. Dad wouldn't worry. He'd get madder, but he wouldn't worry. Uncle Edward called back later and said everything was OK, and he hoped Mr. Eberhart could accommodate his guest overnight, and we'd all talk in the morning.

Mr. Eberhart put me in a tiny room off his kitchen, in a little old bed that creaked. He piled the quilts up on me, in case I kept on feeling cold all the time—and three of his cats came and slept on the bed with me, which helped. We were all very compatible and comfortable. He left a fire going in the old stove in the kitchen, and a small light burning—which was really nice because even someone my age can feel kind of spooked sleeping in a totally dark place they don't know.

I knew I was never going home again, but I tried not to think about it too much in case I cried in front of Mr. Eberhart.

Mr. Eberhart got me up Sunday morning and gave me breakfast. We talked—but not about my walking out. Mostly we talked about gardening. Then Uncle Edward called and asked us to come over around eleven. Mr. Eberhart said yes, but I said no. So Mr. Eberhart got me to promise not to leave till he got back, and he went.

I sat there in the kitchen with the cats, and thought about things. I was feeling pretty bad. The cats kept jumping up into my lap, or rubbing up against my leg—trying to make me feel better. I didn't fit in at school. I didn't fit in at home. My own father couldn't stand me. My Indian stuff was gone, and who knew when it would come back—if ever. My one hope for a place of my own was shot down. By now, the tipi poles were probably at the town dump. And I'd spent almost all my money for the stuff to finish the tipi—so I had no grubstake, except the little left in the bank for karate lessons. I felt about as down and out as I ever had. All I could see, when I closed my eyes, was Dad, taking a swing at me.

I heard Mr. Eberhart's pickup door slam—very tinny—and I looked out. He'd brought back Rodger Dodger and Uncle Edward. I figured he'd sold me out. The state police were probably on the way, was how I figured it. I started out the back door, moving very quietly, very carefully, and just as I thought I was in the clear, someone got me from behind and took me down. Rodger Dodger. He said, "An old Indian trick," and helped me up. He brought me back into the kitchen and said, "Sit down and listen, twit. You might learn something."

I sat down, but I didn't plan to listen. No way.

Well, Rodger Dodger started talking, and he said he had kept my Indian artifacts so long because they were being appraised by the university archaeology department, and they had done their best to figure when everything was made, and by whom, and the big news was that they had decided that my things had been made and left behind by lots of Indians, living in our area over a very long stretch of time. So—they were going to include my things in a special showing of local

Indian artifacts, and mine would have a plaque attached: From the Collection of Mark Anthony Crowder. Rodger and Uncle Edward had kept it real quiet till they knew for sure it would all work out, because, Uncle Edward said, "Once was enough," whatever he meant by that.

So—my stuff was important. I couldn't believe it. And Rodger said that they'd be taking pictures, and if I could get the tipi ready in time, they'd want pictures of that, because I *had* done it right. It was really authentic. He said that I would be invited to a special showing of the exhibit, the night before it opened, and my family could all come, too.

I said "Thanks" a lot, but that was about it. Then I remembered that the tipi was probably already down at the dump and not likely to go up again.

Uncle Edward said, "The tipi still stands, Mark Anthony. Your father picked up the two poles that he'd helped pull down, and he put them back up, himself."

I guess I looked as if I didn't believe him.

Uncle Edward said, "I started to help him, and he waved me off. He sent Mr. Leyden home, and he worked on the tipi himself."

Naturally, I wanted to know why.

Uncle Edward said, "I think it was that moment when he swung at you, and you ran away from him. Have you ever heard of a moment of truth—when someone suddenly wakes up to what's happening, and sees everything clearly? Well, I think he saw things clearly, and now, Mark Anthony, the question is—how clearly do you see him?"

I walked home, alone. Dad was in the living room,

sitting in the wing chair. Just sitting—no lights, no TV. I sat down, too.

He said, "I'm sorry."

I said, "I should have asked—like with the tree house," and that was the truth. I am a slow learner, all right.

He said, "I do my best, Mark Anthony. I do care about you, very much. But most of the time, I just don't understand you. You'll have to talk more to me, and I'll try to listen, or I'll just keep on making this kind of mistake forever. But I do care."

And I said, "I know you do. Listen—they didn't put the squeeze on you about the tipi, did they?"

He said, "No. They did say that you were very, very good at what you like to do. And your mother said she thought you were entitled. And she was right."

It bothered me to see him sitting there, quiet, and kind of down. I couldn't leave the room with him like that. I got up and went over to him and shook his hand. It was a dumb thing to do, but it was all I could think of. Anyhow, it worked. He got up and gave me a little smile, and put his arm around my shoulder and said, "So—let's go and tell your mother the crisis is over, before *she* leaves me."

## Oct. 16

*Oct. 16*—The tipi's up, the exhibit's open—I'm what Uncle Edward calls a ninety-day wonder. Next week, Arnold will go back to heckling me, but he isn't likely to mention Indian collections. Not now. He's got to believe the university. And I start karate lessons next Saturday, so there's hope. I'm still too tall, and my glasses still look like headlight lenses, but I guess I can live with that. Dad and I are trying to talk more. Sometimes I catch him looking at me with his head on one side, as if he was trying to figure me out. But if both of us keep trying, something will get through.

I'm getting older, and Uncle Edward was right—it does get better.